Closer

Also From Kylie Scott

Lies

Repeat

It Seemed Like a Good Idea at the Time

Trust
Lies

THE DIVE BAR SERIES
Dirty
Twist
Chaser

THE STAGE DIVE SERIES
Lick
Play
Lead
Deep
Strong: A Stage Dive Novella

THE FLESH SERIES
Flesh
Skin
Flesh Series Novellas

Heart's a Mess

Colonist's Wife

Closer

A Stage Dive Novella
By Kylie Scott

1001 Dark Nights

EVIL EYE
CONCEPTS

Closer
A Stage Dive Novella
By Kylie Scott

Copyright 2019 Kylie Scott
ISBN: 978-1-970077-05-6

Foreword: Copyright 2014 M.J. Rose

Published by Evil Eye Concepts, Incorporated

Sign up for the 1001 Dark Nights Newsletter
and be entered to win a Tiffany Key necklace.

There's a contest every month!

Go to www.1001DarkNights.com to subscribe.

**As a bonus, all subscribers can download
FIVE FREE exclusive books!**

ONE THOUSAND AND ONE DARK NIGHTS

Once upon a time, in the future...

*I was a student fascinated with stories and learning.
I studied philosophy, poetry, history, the occult, and
the art and science of love and magic. I had a vast
library at my father's home and collected thousands
of volumes of fantastic tales.*

*I learned all about ancient races and bygone
times. About myths and legends and dreams of all
people through the millennium. And the more I read
the stronger my imagination grew until I discovered
that I was able to travel into the stories... to actually
become part of them.*

*I wish I could say that I listened to my teacher
and respected my gift, as I ought to have. If I had, I
would not be telling you this tale now.
But I was foolhardy and confused, showing off
with bravery.*

*One afternoon, curious about the myth of the
Arabian Nights, I traveled back to ancient Persia to
see for myself if it was true that every day Shahryar
(Persian: شهریار, "king") married a new virgin, and then
sent yesterday's wife to be beheaded. It was written
and I had read, that by the time he met Scheherazade,
the vizier's daughter, he'd killed one thousand
women.*

*Something went wrong with my efforts. I arrived
in the midst of the story and somehow exchanged
places with Scheherazade — a phenomena that had
never occurred before and that still to this day, I
cannot explain.*

*Now I am trapped in that ancient past. I have
taken on Scheherazade's life and the only way I can
protect myself and stay alive is to do what she did to
protect herself and stay alive.*

*Every night the King calls for me and listens as I spin tales.
And when the evening ends and dawn breaks, I stop at a
point that leaves him breathless and yearning for more.
And so the King spares my life for one more day, so that
he might hear the rest of my dark tale.*

*As soon as I finish a story... I begin a new
one... like the one that you, dear reader, have before
you now.*

CHAPTER ONE

I couldn't have been more tired if I tried. It felt like a billion hours of traveling cross country for a two-day shoot. And it hadn't helped that I was modelling winter clothes on the streets of New Orleans during the middle of their hot, wet summer. Honest to God, I was ready to lie down and die. Or at least snooze for a really long time, Sleeping Beauty style. Once I got up to my new apartment, of course. After so many years of my life being in a constant state of flux, it was beyond nice to have a home.

"Miss Cooper," said Leonard, the concierge/security guard, with a smile. He was a big strong man in his fifties, if I had to guess. Not someone you'd want to mess with. "Welcome back."

"Thanks."

"How was your trip?"

"Good. How's your week been?"

"Fine, miss," he said. "A parcel came for you. I'll just grab it."

"Thanks, Leonard."

He headed for a door behind the counter as I set my LV Keepall Bandouliére on the floor. One day I would learn not to overpack. Probably not anytime soon, however. I rolled my shoulder back a few times then forward. It didn't help the ache.

Finding exactly the right place to put down roots hadn't been easy. The apartment block sat in the middle of the Pearl District. Right in the heart of a heap of great shops and restaurants. I loved it. New York and Los Angeles might be more fashion world relevant, but Portland was my hometown. Art deco stonework surrounded the front door and the lobby was all shiny surfaces. The building had lots of old world charm. Lots of rock stars too, what with rising star Adam Dillon and half the members of the world famous Stage Dive band taking up the top two floors. They were the cause of occasional fans lurking outside. Thankfully I wasn't the one drawing crowds, which was how I liked it. Live next to someone more famous than yourself and you're bound to be left in peace—most of the time.

Leonard stepped out of the back room with a box in his hands and a frown on his face. "Something's leaking."

"Oh no." A drop of red fell onto the white marble floor. The box was the wrong size for a bottle of wine and I highly doubted someone would have sent me tomatoes. "What the hell?"

He set it on the counter. Several of his fingers were smeared with the stuff. We both stared in growing horror as more of the red stuff oozed from a corner of the unopened box and the scent of copper filled the air.

"I-I think it's blood." I swallowed hard. "Leonard, can you please call the police?"

"I don't want a bodyguard."

"Around about the time someone sends you a dead cow's heart with a knife stabbed through it, you've kind of lost that option." Lena Ferris laid down the law while daintily pushing her red acrylic glasses further up her nose.

She had a point. Not that I was yet ready to admit it. My head fell back against the couch. "But I enjoy being on my own. I like my privacy."

"Oh, please. This is just another side effect of your chosen vocation. You said goodbye to a percentage of privacy when you hit the cover of a certain sports magazine in a tiny black bikini, my dear," she continued. "Five million Instagram followers, some of whom are sending you damn creepy messages, says you need to compromise. It's your safety at stake."

Another valid point from Lena. Dammit.

I'd first met Lena, photographer and wife to the lead singer of Stage Dive, about a year ago on a shoot. We'd bonded immediately. Not only were we both curvy brunettes, we shared a somewhat skewed sense of humor and general appreciation for sarcasm. And given how long and boring shoots can be, the woman was a godsend to work with. It was her recommendation that I look at the apartment that became my home.

"You're not really going to be difficult about this, are you?" she asked, sitting opposite me with a cup of coffee in hand. "I deal enough with big famous babies thanks to my husband and twin daughters."

"No." I sighed. "It's just so…man, it makes me angry that someone gets to mess with my life like this. And I'm too tired to argue with you, especially when I know you're talking sense."

"How much sleep have you had in the last forty-eight hours?"

I sighed. "The detective questioned me until early in the morning. Then, when I finally got up to my apartment, I just kept staring at the bedroom ceiling trying to figure out who'd be deranged enough to do something like this."

"It's probably not someone you know."

"Probably."

"They just think they have a relationship with you because they're crazy."

I frowned. "I mean, an actual heart. It's so gross."

"Agreed," she said. "At any rate, I already called Sam and one of his people is on their way over, so suck it up."

I gave her a small smile. "You know, I do appreciate your help."

"I know. And if someone had sent me a stabbed offal, I'd be upset and angry and all cranky-pants too."

"If this doesn't make me a vegetarian, I'll be heartily surprised. Get it? Heartily."

Lena just gave me a look.

"Bad joke. I know. It was good of your friend to find me someone so fast."

"Sam gets that the situation is urgent. He's one of the good ones. He'd have to be to put up with Martha. She's not exactly low maintenance." Her cell phone chimed. After reading a text message, she grinned and her fingers moved across the screen. "Jimmy wants to know what I'm wearing."

"What are you telling him?"

"A skimpy red silk nightie and a naughty smile."

"You two are so happy and in love." I sighed. Jealousy was a bitch. "I'm sick of you living your best life."

"Sorry. Not."

"Makes me almost miss being in a relationship."

"Ooh, I could set you up with someone! There's this guy–"

"No, thank you."

"Spoilsport. You ruin everything, dude."

"Awesome. Thanks for the feedback."

Lena snorted and I smiled. A little levity felt damn good. Then someone knocked at the door. Ever so slowly, I dragged my oily-haired, yoga pants-wearing, general mess of a self over to answer. A couple hours of shitty broken sleep and a stalker didn't bring out the best in me. Who could have guessed?

I opened the door and...stopped.

"Miss Cooper?" he asked in a deep voice.

I blinked.

He waited.

Say something. "Ah, yes. Hi. That's me."

Over six foot worth of tall, dark, and devastatingly handsome stood before me. And while I was falling apart, he seemed so put together it hurt. My messy bun and spandex clad ass were not anywhere up to dealing with this today. Whoever he was, he needed to leave and come back another time. Preferably when I was rocking one of my best outfits and actually had a clue. Or had at least had a shower. Deodorant could really only go so far.

"I'm Ziggy Thayer," he said. "Samuel Rhodes sent me over."

"He did?"

"Yes."

"Y-you're going to be my bodyguard?"

"Close protection officer, yes."

"Huh."

He tipped his chin. "Is there a problem, miss?"

"I, um..."

Was there a problem? Hell yes. This was a fucking disaster. My brain refused to function, all synapses had stalled. I didn't know if it was the immaculate black suit, general air of badassery, or his stone-faced expression. But whatever it was, he needed to cease and desist with the hotness immediately. It's not like I wasn't used to being around beautiful people. It's part of my job, after all. And he wasn't even beautiful exactly, but for some reason, I couldn't stop staring.

"Mae, you're being weird. Let him in," ordered Lena from the couch. As friends go, Lena and her bluntness occasionally sucked. This was clearly one of those occasions.

"Sorry." I stepped back, heat creeping up my neck. "Please, come in, Mr. Thayer."

"Ziggy will be fine," he said.

"Oh. Then call me Mae."

"He'll call you Miss Cooper," said Lena. "Don't fight it. We've all tried to train the formality out of him, but it never sticks. Does it, Ziggy?"

Not even a hint of an expression or friendly smile from the man. He took resting bitch face to the next level. "No, ma'am."

"Marines." Lena shrugged. "What can you do?"

I shut the door behind him, feeling all types of awkward. This potent example of the male species was going to follow me around for the bulk of my waking hours? No. Not going to happen. Maybe they had someone else they could send over. Someone who didn't take up so much room or make me stop and stare quite so often. That would be good. Drooling in public was never cool and could play havoc with a girl's lip gloss. Wasn't I dealing with enough? Insert heavy sigh here.

Halfway through my self-indulgent sigh, I managed to convert it into a steadying breath. Because I could pull my shit together and be professional. It would be done. In all likelihood, I just needed to get laid. It'd been months since me and the ex had called it quits, an entirely necessary and mutual decision. I needed to be free, to find some balance when my career and focus changed gears as I hit my thirties. And he apparently needed to be free to have sex with every barely legal football player fangirl who crossed his path. Especially the ones who liked to film themselves having sex with him and post it on the internet. Those were his favorite. Such is life.

Lena raised a hand. "Hey, Ziggy."

"Mrs. Ferris."

"Mae's just tired and a little freaked out. Get her to sleep for a few hours and clean herself up, and she'll be fine."

He said nothing. Just stood there with a flinty gaze.

Meanwhile, I looked around for something to seal Lena's lips shut. For at least the duration of her visit would be nice. Electrical tape maybe. Needle and thread seemed extreme, but not entirely out of the question.

Ziggy cleared his throat. "Miss Cooper, I notice you didn't engage the deadlock or the security system. We'll need to discuss that."

"Ruh roh," said Lena. "You're getting spanked already. That was fast."

My face flamed.

"I better leave you guys to it."

"You're going?" Hard to gauge what I was most afraid of, being left alone with the close protection officer, or waiting to hear what Lena said next. Both, perhaps.

"Jimmy has a big charity thing on tonight. I need to go get myself sorted out." She wandered over and smacked a kiss on my cheek. "Try not to worry, Mae. Everything's going to be fine. Call me if you need anything, okay?"

I managed a smile. "I will. Thank you again."

"Anytime. See you tomorrow."

And she was gone.

Leaving me alone with him.

"So," I said with a hesitant smile. In these situations, normal people with a functioning brain were often polite. Maybe I should try it out. "Shall we sit? Can I get you a drink?"

"No, thank you, miss."

That was really going to take some getting used to. Being called "miss" all the time.

He took the freshly vacated seat opposite me, sitting on the edge of the couch. Ready to launch into action at any moment, no doubt. Everything about him screamed big, scary, and capable. Though I'm sure he was a nice guy at heart. Probably an absolute delight at parties. Loved puppies and made origami cranes in his spare time. Or maybe not. I sat and curled my feet up beneath me, making myself as small a target as possible. Guess I was just feeling vulnerable for some reason. Not that I was afraid of him or anything. Hell no. Just because.

I squared my shoulders and sat up straighter. "So…where do we start?"

CHAPTER TWO

I'd had bodyguards before. But only for events like fashion week or a big shoot. Just for a limited amount of time. My contract with Ziggy, however, was open ended, dependent on the heart in the box situation. Once he'd grilled me about what the police were doing (investigating my entire life), my routine (I don't really have one. It's consumed by work), and my calendar for the next few days (I'd freed up time to finish unpacking and then back to work on my lingerie line), he drove me to the gym. There was one I used a couple of times in the apartment building, but I generally do better with some active encouragement and guidance.

Guess Ziggy approved of my Land Rover because he gave it another one of those almost-smiles. I, however, continued to receive the full professional cold front face. This was definitely going to take some getting used to.

"Who's your shadow?" asked Kwana, my awesome trainer.

I paused mid-lunge, my breath coming hard and fast. "My bodyguard, Ziggy. You like him?"

"He's pretty. Don't stop, keep moving."

"Yeah, yeah."

"You don't usually have one of them around. Have you been getting hassled or something?"

Kwana stood with her arms crossed, all lean muscles beneath brown skin. Since we were in an open area at the end of the main part of the gym, Ziggy waited over by the wall, just out of earshot. He stood with his arms loose at his side, his gaze constantly wandering a circuit from me—around the room, over to the exits, and back again. Always on alert.

"More a precaution than anything," I said.

No matter how much I liked Kwana, no one outside my inner circle needed to know about the incident. The fewer people who found out about the gross cow heart and knife the better.

There'd been no further news from the police. Though it was never likely they'd track down a suspect and charge that person the next day.

Case closed, hooray!

I wish. It'd take them weeks to go through my correspondence. I shuddered at the thought. For years I'd received weird and smutty emails and messages from all sorts of people. Believe me, my collection of unasked for and unwanted dick pics was epic. Why random dudes thought I wanted to see their hairy little balls and pecker I have no idea. But it was all just part of putting yourself out there as a woman these days. Land on the cover of some magazines and it only gets worse.

And now some poor cops would have to wade through it, dick pics and all. Maybe in time they'd do a lineup of the usual suspects, and get them all to drop their trousers for a positive ID. Or some computer database would bring up a match based on the culprit's short and curlies. I could just imagine the CSI episode now.

Kwana sniffed. "Fine. Don't tell me. Move on to squats."

"Lady, you're mean."

"You love it."

"True." I wiped the sweat off my face with the back of my hand and kept going. "I wouldn't call him pretty exactly."

"Masculine pretty," amended Kwana. "It's that angular jawline and cut yourself cheekbones. Gets me every time. Move faster. Come on, you're not even trying."

"My life hurts," I whined, but did as told. The woman was going to kill me.

She lowered her voice, taking a step closer. "He's looking at you."

"Who, Ziggy? It's his job to look at me."

"No. I mean, his eyes were on your ass. Hell, they were glued to those globes."

I snorted. "I'm sure you're mistaken."

"I most certainly am not."

A man in fluorescent workout gear approached from over by the dumbbells. Before I'd even finished registering him, Ziggy was there, putting himself between us. The guy held out a scrap of paper and pen, face a mixture of "c'mon, man" and "please." Ziggy just shook his head.

"Can't you see she's busy here?" Kwana scowled. "Ask for an autograph later."

"No autographs." Ziggy's tone was final. "Only at official engagements."

With a heavy scowl, the dude stomped off toward an elliptical machine.

"We're back in the private room next time," said my trainer.

I nodded. "Might be best."

"Heel raises, please."

"Man," I bitched. It was an important part of my workout process.

"Oh, just do it." Kwana sighed. "You want those calves looking good when you wear your fancy shoes, don't you?"

"Yes."

"Get on with it then. One of these days I'm going to start charging extra every time you complain." In all honesty, the woman deserved the money. I was a whiny baby when it came to exercise. She lightly placed her hands on my shoulders. "That's it, Mae. Nice and slow. Get up high."

I concentrated on my breathing and balance, ignoring the burning in my leg muscles. It was all for a good cause. Soon enough the happy exercise hormones would kick in and I'd be glad for the effort. Hopefully. It was all part of the job, along with extensive waxing, facials, manicures, hair, lashes, massages, and a beauty routine to end all others. Just because I wasn't size zero (or even close) didn't mean I could get away with being unfit or lacking in the rest. Shoots could be grueling enough, let alone if your energy levels were low or you were behind on maintenance. Trust me, being yelled at by a stressed-out designer because you didn't bring your best to the show was not fun. Also, word got around. For such a big industry, it could be amazingly small at times.

"You're doing great. Keep going." Kwana's gaze jumped to the front wall of windows behind me. They faced the street. A frown crossed her face.

"What's wrong?"

"Paparazzi are outside."

She was right. They were crowded up against the glass with their cameras. A whole feral pack of them. Shit. Meanwhile, Ziggy had his cell pressed against his ear. A faint frown crossed his face as he watched the mass of people gathering at the window.

My stomach sank. "Is there anyone else here?"

"No one they'd be interested in," said Kwana.

"Guess we're almost finished anyway. Sorry about this."

Ziggy strode toward us, slipping his cell into his jacket pocket. "We should go before more arrive."

"Someone leaked the story, didn't they?" I asked.

"It looks that way."

I hung my head and swore silently.

"You get the car, we'll meet you at the back door," said Kwana. "No one will get near her. You can trust me. This isn't my first famous person rodeo."

For a moment, Ziggy hesitated. Then he nodded and jogged toward the now crowded front door.

"All right, Mae, let's get your bag." Kwana ushered me into the women's locker room. Only one woman was in there, patiently applying mascara at the mirror. She didn't show any particular interest in us.

I grabbed my hoodie out of my bag and put it on. Sunglasses too. It probably wouldn't help. But it couldn't hurt. In all honesty, hoping my stalker situation wouldn't get out had probably been a fantasy. I might not be as well-known as others, but give social media a slow news cycle and they'd be more than happy to pick my life apart for a moment's entertainment. Nothing I could do about it.

Kwana led me through a back corridor to the rear exit.

"So who are your other famous clients?" I asked, trying to get my mind off the mess waiting outside.

"Hmm? Oh, I sign N.D.A.s. I'm not allowed to talk about it." She opened the door just a little, peering out at the fading afternoon light. "But let me just say that a certain drummer is banned from this gym for life. The idiot."

"What did he do?"

"I already told you, I can't say," she said, distracted by whatever was going on outside. "Here comes your buff bodyguard and a couple of paps are following. Get ready."

"Thanks. See you next time."

"Sure, hon."

The car pulled up close to the building with the passenger side right in front of me. I raced out. Flashes went off, but I kept a hand up, covering part of my face. They weren't getting a good shot of me today. Not under these circumstances. So there.

Inside the car, everything was quiet apart from the pounding of my heart. Ziggy drove fast but skillfully through the city streets. Usually I liked being out and about after dark. People out having fun, the sight of street lights rushing past. It all soothed me for some reason. Probably due to childhood memories of Mom picking me up from Grandma's place and driving me home late at night after her shift at the bar. But nothing could relax me this evening.

"No need to rush," I said. "They know where we're going. One of the downsides to living under half of Stage Dive. Everyone in the area knows about that building."

He slowed a little.

"With no time for a shower, I must smell amazing."

Another of those almost-smiles tugged at his lips. "You're fine, miss."

"Guess someone at the police station either talked or sold the story. I can't imagine Leonard or anyone else at the apartment building doing it."

"I know the people who work at your building. No way would it have been one of them."

"Good," I said. "That makes me feel a little better."

"Speaking of which…" With more multitasking skill than I could ever display, he drew out his cell and made a call. "Hey, Sarah, it's Ziggy. Miss Cooper and I are coming in with photographers on our tail. Just giving you warning…right. Thanks."

"They're at the building too, already?" I asked.

"Yes."

Not a surprise. But it still sucked. Behind us, paparazzi followed on motorbikes, scooters, and in cars. A whole bunch of them. Oh man, this was just fucking great. No, wait, hold up. I needed an attitude adjustment. Enough with the moping and fretting. Especially since it wouldn't help a damn thing. Deep breath. This too would pass. A few days and no doubt they'd be talking about someone else, and my stalker would be behind bars. This would all be over and I could go back to my normal life of coming and going as I pleased. After all, it couldn't be any worse than when my idiot cheating ex's sex tape hit the internet and I survived that. I'd been working in New York and all of the attention during that emotionally upsetting time was an unhelpful pain in the ass, and then some.

The gates to the underground parking garage beneath my building clanged shut behind us and I breathed a sigh of relief. "You might as well head home. I'll be staying in for the rest of the night."

"I'll see you upstairs and check your apartment. Then I'll be on my way."

"But the building has security." I undid my seatbelt. "You think that's really necessary?"

"Yes, miss."

I exhaled. Chin up, shoulders back, tits out. Time to pull my shit together and make my mom proud. "Okay then."

He went before me, first checking that the elevator was empty, then he checked the hall outside my apartment.

"Your keys and security alarm code please, miss?" he asked, hand held out waiting.

It might have just been me, but we seemed to be standing awfully close together. It almost seemed weirdly intimate. Almost. No, my bad. Ziggy wore his usual professional façade with nary a hint of emotion on display. His gaze was shuttered, his bearing military rigid. It was definitely just me and my overactive imagination. Being vaguely attracted to your bodyguard was kind of a pain in the ass. Not that I couldn't use the distraction right now.

Ziggy continued to stand there patiently waiting.

"Keys. Right." I rummaged inside my Balenciaga City bag. Designer goodies were not only a weakness of mine, but a happy perk of being in the industry and achieving some small fame. "Ah, just a minute. They're in here somewhere."

I pushed aside my purse, a cashmere shawl, tampons, a candy bar, some loose change, my small Chanel cosmetics case, a power bank, hair ties, pepper spray, a copy of the latest Sarah MacLean book, mints, a spare charging cable for my cell phone, the cell phone itself, Chapstick, Prada sunglasses case, my grandma's rosary, dental floss, deodorant, a couple of pens, Kleenex, ear buds, water bottle, a USB stick, reusable straw, condoms, nail file, some old receipts, a travel size umbrella, hand sanitizer, lotion, a pair of pearl earrings, tweezers, Advil, a hair band, and some bobby pins.

"Sorry about this," I murmured. "I know I put them in here when we left."

He said nothing. A whole lot of nothing.

"Huh." With a great sense of victory, I held up a bottle of nail polish. "I thought I'd lost this."

One of his dark brows crept upwards.

"I'll have you know this color was limited edition. Little Death at Midnight by Oxley. You can't buy it anymore."

His lips did not move, but that damn eyebrow arched even higher as he leaned forward a little and took in the contents of my bag. I swear his eyes widened.

"Don't you judge me. All of these things are necessary for my ongoing existence."

"Of course they are, miss." The man was so judging me. Bastard. "You carry a koozie around with you, I see."

"It pays to be ready to party, Mr. Thayer." I finally produced the keys, dangling on a Miss Piggy fob. "Here you go. Alarm code is eight five star three zero one two."

"Yours and your mother's birthdays?"

"How on earth do you know that?"

"We have extensive files on all our clients."

"I haven't been your client for that long."

"We also do background checks for the owner of the building." He unlocked the door and punched in the code before standing aside so I could enter. The door was then locked behind me.

"That would explain it. Still, you have a very good memory."

"That code will need to be changed to something random," he said. "And it might be best if I hang on to the keys next time. Should there be an incident, we don't want anything delaying you from getting into a secure location. If you could wait here please, miss."

He strode through my apartment, giving it a thorough, if fast, inspection. My open plan living room, kitchen, dining space, office, spare bedroom, bathroom, and…this was exactly when it occurred to me.

"Wait!" Sore calves or not, I ran. "Ziggy, stop!"

Brows drawn in tight, he stood in my bedroom. "Please wait back at the door until I've cleared the apartment."

"Just give me a second."

"Miss Cooper," he said.

"Just give me one second."

"I must insist."

With one hand I scooped up the underwear, T-shirt, cardigan, jeans, and shoes I'd worn yesterday. "Normally I tidy up after myself and make my bed, I swear. This is very unusual for me."

He just blinked.

"I just got in so early in the morning and then I slept so badly," I said in an almighty rush. "Please don't think I'm a slob."

He blinked again. "There are precisely six locations in this room that an intruder could hope to hide in. That is all I'm thinking about."

"Okay." I smiled. "Good. Stick with that."

His movements somewhat more stilted than before, he checked in my ensuite and extensive walk-in closet.

"Well, that wasn't embarrassing at all," I said. "All clear?"

"Yes."

"Great. Excellent."

The man just looked at me. I'm not sure what the look meant. But then his gaze dropped to the collection of items in my arms. Most noticeably, to the black lace thong dangling off my finger. Oops. Quick as possible, I scrunched it up in my hand. Out of sight, out of mind, right? Might have been the low lighting, yet I could have sworn the man almost blushed.

"Guess you've seen just about everything, what with being a bodyguard." I slapped on my best friendliest smile. He wasn't the only one who knew how to strike a pose. Even if his poses were mostly imitations of rock formations and other impassive, poker-faced things.

"Yes, miss."

"Probably seen people doing all sorts of crazy things. My messy bedroom probably doesn't even really rate."

Another blink.

"You know, men usually have to take me out to dinner before they get to see my underwear," I joked.

The man just stared.

Oh, God. "I shouldn't have said that. That was really inappropriate. I'm so sorry. When I get nervous I tend to blather and nothing that comes out is ever any good."

"It's fine, miss."

"I'm usually much more together than this. I don't–"

"I'm going to leave now."

I took a breath. "Um, yeah. That might be for the best."

"If you could be sure to lock the door after me and use the security system?"

"Of course. Sorry again."

He turned to go, then paused, a flash of irritation crossing his face. "I forgot to ask, have you decided upon your movements tomorrow?"

"Nothing much until my lunch appointment."

"I'll be here at nine then. There's a few jobs I'd like to do before we head out."

"Okay."

And I definitely did not imagine his gaze returning to the hand holding my black silk thong. It was for the briefest of moments. If I blinked, I would have missed it. But I didn't. Maybe I'd scarred the man for life by inadvertently flashing my underwear. Maybe he couldn't believe what a train wreck I was. Or maybe he just liked looking at women's lingerie. I don't know.

Then he was gone. Ziggy sure could move fast when motivated.

Generally speaking, I didn't tend to go around scaring grown men. Especially not former Marines. Though I wasn't sure how else to interpret what just happened. Down the hallway, the front door clicked shut and I sighed. Maybe he'd send someone else tomorrow. He'd have to be a brave man to come back for more.

CHAPTER THREE

"Morning, Ziggy."

"Morning, Miss Cooper."

Giant-ass size mug of coffee in hand, I shuffled back into the spare bedroom, where an abundance of packing boxes awaited. "Are the hordes still downstairs?"

"Yes, they are."

"Great. Must be a slow news week."

And details of my gruesome bloody delivery had indeed spread everywhere. Having been bombarded with messages and calls, I'd made the smart decision to mute my cell. After first posting a behind-the-scenes picture from the recent shoot in New Orleans on Instagram and calling my mom, of course. She'd been horrified and pressed to come stay with me. I barely managed to convince her it wasn't necessary. I needed some space to deal with things right now and having Ziggy and all his hotness in my face was already more than I could handle. I knew my mom would take over the place with a lot of good intentions but not much awareness of my slowly growing freak-out, barely being kept under control.

No, thank you.

Also, she had enough going on planning her wedding to Dr. Jane next month. A wonderful woman, and they made a great couple. Mom deserved much happiness after all those years of raising me on her own. Teenage girls could be hellacious and I'd been no exception. So many hormones bouncing around inside. Besides which, girls could be mean. It had been a tough time for everyone.

And speaking of hotness getting all up in my face, my bodyguard looked as slick as ever in his obviously custom-tailored black suit. Guess carrying a gun around in a holster necessitated the tailoring. I, on the other hand, wore my favorite boyfriend jeans, an old Ramones tee, messy bun, and concealer to hide the sleep deprivation bruising beneath my eyes. I had at least showered. Bonus points to me.

"Will you still be going to lunch with Mrs. Ferris?" he asked.

I cocked my head. "What's your professional opinion? I'd been looking forward to it. There's this cool new place we were going to try. But…"

"I won't lie to you. Crowds massively increase the amount of moving parts in your environment. You never know who or what might be hiding in them. And right now, you're bound to have people following wherever you go."

"Hmm."

"It's my job to assess threats and keep you safe." His cell started to vibrate somewhere about his person. He pulled it out of his back pants pocket, checked the screen, and dismissed the call with a slide of his thumb. "But only you can decide what risk is important enough, for whatever reason, to be worth taking."

"If they're all still out there then I guess I might cancel my plans." I planted my ass on the carpet and picked up my cell, sending Lena a quick text to let her know. Given the situation, I cancelled my appointment with my hairdresser in the afternoon as well. "Looks like I'm spending the day at home. You probably don't need to hang around."

"You won't be leaving your apartment at all?"

"Only maybe to go down to the apartment building's gym later."

"Then I'll stay. There're some other tasks I have to do while you're busy here."

I opened my mouth to argue, but then changed my mind. After a long night of jumping at every little noise, keeping the bodyguard around might be for the best. Calm the savage nerves and all that. If it was a choice between annoying hotness and crippling fear, then I'll go for the heat every time. "Okay."

"Any update from Detective Ortega?"

"No. Not a word." I sighed. "I tried going through some of my emails and messages last night, to see if they mentioned hearts or knives or anything like that. There's some seriously deranged people out there. I mean, can you imagine sending a message to a complete stranger saying that baby Jesus was going to strike them down dead and send them to hell? Or that you wanted to strangle them and have sex with their corpse? Who the hell says that sort of thing? Just because they can hide behind a bullshit email address or fake avatar they think they can let all of their ugly out to play and inflict it on other people."

His gaze narrowed, lines furrowing his brow. "Why don't you let the police deal with that in the future, Miss Cooper? You don't need that sort of shit getting into your head. Excuse my language."

I attempted a smile. "It's fine. Swear all you like. This situation makes me want to swear too."

"There's a lot of sick and cruel people out there. It doesn't mean you need to give them a moment of your time."

"True," I said. "I guess you've seen a lot of this sort of stuff before."

"Enough to know you're better off staying away from it and leaving the detective work to the professionals."

"I know, I know." My shoulders slumped, my back bowed. My bones felt hollow and weak. Tonight I'd take some Melatonin and try to knock myself out. Actually get some decent sleep. "I just hate being so out of control. Having to put my life on pause because of this asshole."

"Understandable."

Around me were towers of books waiting to be shelved. Romance mostly. Since I had the time, I might as well place them in alphabetical order. His gaze wandered over them with something close to interest. Made me curious about his hobbies. Apart from being a fulltime card-carrying member of the badass club, of course. He probably kick boxed and scaled tall buildings and saved kittens from burning trees. I really shouldn't have sat down. From this height, he seemed even more imposing. Like a mountain towering over me, taking up all of the view. I'd been around plenty of big shot actors, sports stars, and business tycoons over the years, courtesy of various events and V.I.P. lounges. Ziggy Thayer had more presence than all of them put together. It's like he sucked the air out of a room just by generally being cool and existing.

Or maybe he only had that effect on me. If so, I could seriously do without the complication. Dammit.

"Miss?"

And I'd been staring at the man again. "I'm sorry, Ziggy. I kind of zoned out there for a minute. Were you saying something?"

"Only that I better get on with it. I'll be down in the garage. If you need me, just contact me on my cell."

"Why the garage?" I asked, curious.

"I'd like to give your vehicle a quick check over, followed by your apartment."

His phone started to vibrate again.

"Do you need to take that call?"

"No, miss."

"What are you looking for in my car and apartment?"

"Anything that shouldn't be there. Listening devices, mostly."

"You think that the crazy person who mailed me a skewered heart might be bugging my car? Psycho nut does Mission Impossible?"

"No. My concern is with the press."

I paused. "You think someone might have been listening into my conversations and that's how the story got leaked?"

"It's highly unlikely," he said. "But I'd feel better if I checked and since I have the time..."

"All right. And thank you for listening to me moan before."

"Anytime, miss. It's all part of the service." The skin around his eyes crinkled a little. It might be the closest thing to a grin I'd ever see on his face.

It made me smile for real.

He nodded as if pleased, then stalked off. The man was like a big jungle cat. I'd sauntered and strutted down plenty of walkways. But away from that world, I was more likely to stub my toe on a coffee table than move with any particular grace. Ziggy's movements seemed innate. A quintessential part of him. Guess they probably trained you in the military to stand tall and walk like you mean it and everything. Kind of made me wonder how he did other things. Private things I had no business thinking about. I needed to stop sexually harassing the man inside my head. It was bad and wrong and I should know better. I really should.

A couple of hours later, Ziggy stood in front of my kitchen island, taking in the array of food on display. His eyes were the size of plates.

Guess I'd impressed him. My chocolate cake, brownies, and chocolate chip cookies sure impressed me. And chocolate was important for any sort of balanced diet. After all, I was a growing girl (spiritual growth mattered) who needed to keep her strength up to deal with the harsh realities of life and douchebags on the internet. After half an hour or so of book sorting, I needed to change activities. Maybe I had a case of the overtired freaked-out hysterics. But I had to be up and on my feet doing something and moving around. I had a killer of a sweet tooth so that made the decision easy.

"I stress bake. It's kind of my thing," I explained, wiping my hands on my apron. "Are you hungry? Do you like sweet things?"

"I love sweet things."

"Excellent. Take a seat."

He sat on one of the stools on the opposite side of the island, watching me serve him a fork along with a plate containing one of everything. The small walkie talkie looking type thing he'd been using to search for listening devices lay in front of him.

"Did you find anything?" I asked.

"No."

"That's good to know. Did you know desserts taste better when eaten with a fork?"

"Is that a fact?"

"Absolutely. Try it and see. The only caveat is to not attempt it with ice cream or pudding. That can get messy," I said. "Milk or coffee?"

"Water will be fine. Thank you, Miss Cooper."

I grabbed him a glass from the jug in the fridge then stood opposite him, eating my own slice of chocolate frosting covered heaven. How could you be down when you had cake? It was impossible. Ziggy ate with an economy and efficiency of movement. Not shoving it in like an animal, but not wasting time either.

"It's good," he said.

I smiled. "So what's your job like?"

He did a one shoulder shrug. "It's a job. It's what I'm trained for."

"You never wanted to do anything else?"

"Not really. Enlisted straight out of school then moved into close protection work once I left the Marines. What about you?"

"A modeling agent approached me at an airport when I was nineteen. Mom and I had just been on an epic trip to Disneyland for her fortieth birthday. We had such a good time." I used my fork to carefully cut off another small piece of cake. Truth was, after all the cookie dough I'd digested, I wasn't actually hungry. So I guess stress baking and comfort eating were two of my things. "I'd been working, saving my pennies, and hanging out with friends. But who wouldn't want to be part of the glamour, getting to wear cool clothes and travel the world?"

"Is that what it's like?"

"Sometimes," I said. "But more often than not, it's boring and awkward and working long hours. You get to travel, but it's rare that you actually get to do any sightseeing. Things tend to be pretty rushed on business trips. And when you're starting out you have to stay in the model apartments. Imagine twelve people, some of whom have seriously dodgy hygiene, squeezed into a three-bedroom dump and paying through the roof for it half the damn time. Ugh. Listen to me whine."

He did the solo brow raise thing. Such a cool move. "How is modeling awkward?"

"Have you never been backstage at a fashion show?"

"Can't say I have."

"T and A as far as the eye can see. I used to be shy and demure, dammit!"

This time it was definitely there. The small twitch of his lips revealing the faintest of smiles. If it wouldn't have been obvious and embarrassing, I'd have high-fived myself in victory. I made Ziggy Thayer's tough guy stone façade crack for a second. Go me. Even dead tired and half falling apart, this was something to celebrate. With more chocolate cake, of course.

He gave me a long hard look. I'd have paid real money to know what he was thinking. Lucky for me, I didn't have to. This time at least.

"Had to escort a group of businessmen around a bunch of sex clubs once. That was eye-opening," he said. "And then there was a member of royalty who was into being watched and walked in on. You couldn't enter a room without accidentally catching sight of something."

"Oh my God. How did you keep a straight face?"

"Keeping a straight face is one of my specialties."

"I've noticed."

There it was again. His lips curved upward by about an eighth of an inch. Maybe less. One thing was for sure, my eyesight would be sharp as hell by the time this man left to protect someone else.

"All of this sangfroid of yours makes me want to say weird and outrageous things just to try and catch you off guard," I confessed. "But I'll do my best to try to restrain myself. Today at least."

"I appreciate that."

"You're very welcome." I grinned. Holy cow. Were we flirting? Or was it just me and my overactive imagination?

"Miss Cooper," he said in that rough low voice. "When's the last time you slept? I mean really slept."

"Do I look that bad?"

"You look fine. But you do look like you could use a decent night's sleep."

I turned away, embarrassed for some reason. Teary almost. Actually I completely knew the reason. Being worn out and having someone you liked call you on it kind of sucked. No matter how nice he was trying to be.

"This stalker thing and the messages and everything have got me a little...wound up, I guess," I said. "Jittery, you know? Actually, you probably don't know. I can't imagine anything scaring you."

"You'd be wrong about that."

I said nothing.

"I never had any trouble sleeping in Afghanistan, but as soon as I returned stateside, it just all hit me. I don't know if it was too quiet after being over there or what. But any little sound woke me up. I'd just be lying there wide awake and on edge. And the dreams..."

I didn't know what to say.

"Also my dad was a truck driver and Mom used to hate it when he was away. Always said she couldn't sleep a wink." His gaze softened. "She wasn't weak or frail. Trust me, no one wants to cross Mom when she's in a mood. But she liked knowing someone else was there to help out if anything went wrong, I think. That she didn't have to face things alone."

"I can see that."

"Do you think maybe you could lie down and take an afternoon nap while I'm here?"

I exhaled, untying the apron strings. "I suppose I could try."

"Good."

I packed up the baked goods while Ziggy went back to checking the apartment with the little black box thingy. Normally an afternoon nap was holiday behavior. A luxury item. I closed the curtains in my room and toed off my shoes. My king-size bed happened to be one of my all-time favorite places to be. Silvery gray pillows and comforter with a mattress that was to die for. I rolled onto my side and shut my eyes. Everything seemed strangely quiet. With the bedroom door closed, I couldn't hear Ziggy's footsteps in the main room. No taps were dripping, though the A.C. did click off and on. It wasn't as dark as during the night, but I still felt weirdly vulnerable all curled up on my bed. Like someone was watching or something. Not a sensation I enjoyed.

If only my brain would shut up and shut down. That would be nice. Instead, it kept regurgitating the content of those horrible disturbing emails. When I was busy, I'd mostly been able to keep it out of my head. But not now. What kind of asshole would threaten a complete stranger? After my breakup, I'd been inundated with emails from his fans calling me a disloyal frigid bitch, among other charming epithets. They threatened me with all sorts of awful things. For a while I just deleted any message sent by a stranger. People could be such trash. Generally speaking, I tried to see the good in the world and all the people contained therein. However, some people were just oxygen bandits.

Then there was Ziggy and all he'd told me. I had so many questions about his life that I'd have loved to ask the man. If he'd talked to someone about his experiences when he got back from the Middle East. If he was okay. But we weren't friends, no matter how cordial he'd been. I didn't want to risk crossing any lines and having him stop talking to me. Not when he was maybe sort of starting to trust me a little.

Oh, man. This was hopeless. I got up and trudged over to the door. It was kind of Ziggy to try and help, but it hadn't worked. Perhaps by tonight I'd be ready to collapse into unconsciousness. Pull a Sleeping Beauty and be out for an eon or two. Sooner or later I surely had to crash. Surely.

He was checking the locks on the glass door leading out onto the balcony. "No good?"

"No. Thanks anyway."

"Go lie back down."

"What?"

He set the doodad down on the kitchen counter. "I want to try something. Go and lie back down."

"Mr. Thayer, what exactly are you planning to do?"

"Miss Cooper, please."

I huffed somewhat crankily and headed back into my bedroom. "Fine. Okay. But whatever it is, it's not going to work."

"I appreciate your open mindedness."

"Very funny."

He followed me into the room, sitting in the charcoal velvet wingback against the wall. Plenty of distance away from my big bed though facing toward me. This was crazy town. And sadly, he didn't plan on indulging in any naked shenanigans.

"I don't think you watching me is going to help me relax," I said.

"Let's just try and see."

I lay down, trying to get comfortable. But tranquil and relaxed wasn't how I felt around my current crush. Stupid libido. Why couldn't I just respect him for his mind? So shallow of me. "Isn't this a bit above and beyond the tenets of your position?"

"Quiet time now."

"Are you telling me to shut up?"

He sighed more heavily than any put-upon male has ever felt the need to sigh before. Truly it was mighty. "Mae. Please…"

"Alright, alright," I said, getting settled. "But only because you used my first name."

"You have to close your eyes."

I did as told. "Are you going to tell me a bedtime story?"

"No." And he said no more.

I opened one eye, just to check on the situation. But he was sitting there, watching me in silence. What with my job and all, people staring at me happened on a regular basis. However, having this man's full attention was something else indeed. He looked at me and I looked at him, and neither of us said anything. Apparently the man would just be waiting me out.

Fine. Whatever.

I closed my watchful eye and laced my fingers over my belly. No chance I'd actually fall asleep like this, no matter how tired I was. It had been a while since anyone was in my bedroom, let alone watched me sleep. Not sure if it was more of a stalker or a safety blanket move. Though I did feel protected with him there. Also weirded out in a way, but still. Ziggy carried a gun and probably knew how to Kung Fu or

Muay Thai someone into oblivion, whereas I'd flunked out of boxercise. So it's not like anyone would be getting past the man to hurt me. Right here and now I was safe.

With nothing else to listen to, I listened to him breathe. In and out, in and out. Slow and steady. Calm and controlled. And somewhere along the line, miracle of miracles, I actually did drift off to sleep.

CHAPTER FOUR

A knock on the door woke me. Couldn't tell what time it was with the curtains drawn and the room mostly in darkness. But in the corner sat a large dark shadow of a man. I reached for my cell on the bedside table. No way. It said nine am. I'd slept a whole damn day. I flicked on the lamp, yawning and stretching.

Fast asleep, Ziggy didn't seem quite as intimidating. His head lay against the side of the chair. His long dark eyelashes rested against his face. The striking angular lines of his cheekbones were softened somehow. Stubble lined his jaw and the hint of roughness suited him big time. Across his lap lay his suitcoat along with his holster and gun. Bet he'd be up and ready to go in an instant if necessary. Surprising he hadn't heard the knock. He must be fast asleep.

It made my heart mushy, seeing him this way, knowing he'd stayed all night to watch over me. Or maybe he'd been exhausted and had simply crashed for an epic sleep too. Then again, maybe he was just a kind person. A bit of both, perhaps?

The knocking came again and he stirred. I jumped out of bed and ran for the door before the noise could fully wake him, stopping to check the identity of my visitor in the peephole like a sensible person before turning off the alarm.

"Leonard." I smiled.

"Morning, Miss Cooper. Got a delivery for you. It's heavy." He paused so I could extract the card then wandered inside carrying the mountain-sized flower arrangement. Roses, orchids, and lilies among a wealth of other flowers were spilling out all over the place in a riot of colors. "Kitchen counter okay?"

"Yes, thank you."

"It came from a local florist and the sender is a known acquaintance of yours. Hope you don't mind, but I felt it best to check it wasn't the crackpot who sent you that nonsense the other day."

"Oh, good. That's a relief."

"Also, most of the photographers from downstairs are gone."

My shoulders sagged. I hadn't even registered how tightly strung my muscles were until they relaxed. "I'm *very* happy to hear that."

"Have a nice day, ma'am."

"You too."

Leonard headed back out, and I shut things up behind him before turning to the flowers.

"Impressive," said Ziggy, standing in the hallway with his suitcoat back on. "You checked your peephole, ascertained the delivery's status, and then relocked the door and reset the alarm system. That's the security conscious mentality we're aiming for."

I swallowed a bit uncomfortably. Not that I didn't like the praise, but this was weird, waking up to him being in my home. Not bad weird. Just ever so slightly awkward. Intimate in a strange way might be the best explanation. Also, I probably looked a mess.

"Good morning." I braved a smile. "I didn't expect you to stay all night."

"If you haven't seen me leave, then I'll be here. Always. Security breaches happen when the client thinks they have protection but don't." A shrug. "Besides, I didn't want you to wake up alone if you had nightmares or something."

More of the mushy sensation invaded my heart. "Thank you. I appreciate that. Can I get you some coffee?"

"Please."

I turned on the machine, which was all set to go from yesterday. No way would I ever attempt facing the A.M. without serious caffeine running through my veins. Then I opened the card and any and all good feelings faded in an instant. "Ugh. You have to be kidding me. They're from my ex. He's worried about me and misses me, apparently. Should have thought of that before he stuck his dick in places it didn't belong. Wants me to call him. As if. Not today, Satan. Not tomorrow either."

A grunt from Ziggy standing sentry at the end of the counter.

"Sorry. That was an overshare." I sighed, staring at the arrangement. In days of yore there'd been a language to flowers. Meanings for each bloom. Though I'm certain there wasn't a bloom that meant sorry I cheated on you and it got posted on You Tube. Forget-me-nots, maybe. "They're pretty though, don't you think? They smell divine. Would you like them for your mom perhaps? Or your girlfriend or significant other, of course. I just assumed, I never asked if..."

He just blinked.

"Not that it's any of my business."

"Mom's in San Francisco and I'm not seeing anyone currently. Though I appreciate the offer."

I popped the card in the bin. An incinerator would have been preferable, but I could make do. Leave it to the creep of an ex to go so overboard. There weren't enough flowers in all of Oregon to convince me to make that mistake again. Like I'd ever be open to the idea after being so publicly cheated on and humiliated by the man. Not that he was a man. An amoeba, maybe. A dollop of slime on the collective shoe of humanity. Something along those lines. And unfortunately, every time I saw the flowers I'd just be reminded of his existence. Not that I wished him ill. So long as he stayed the hell away from me and didn't attempt contact again, all would be fine and dandy.

"You really don't like him, huh?" asked Ziggy in a low voice.

"Bad break-up. And that's putting it mildly."

"I can get rid of them for you if you like."

"Actually, that would be great."

Ziggy nodded and picked up the Godzilla-sized arrangement. I opened the door for him. "Back in a moment, Miss Cooper."

"I'll have the coffee ready and waiting." Much better. Someone else could enjoy their bright loveliness and gorgeous scent minus the taint of he-who-is-in-the-past-and-shall-not-be-named.

Alone for a minute, I took the opportunity to brush my teeth, run a comb through my hair, and put on some deodorant. My clothes were crumpled. But they could wait for me to be post coffee before I showered and changed.

When he returned, he carried a black duffle in one hand and a suit bag in the other. Guess he'd fetched them from his vehicle. "Would it be all right if I used your bathroom? Otherwise I could use the one down in the building's gym if you'd prefer?"

"No. Please. Make yourself at home."

A nod and he was gone.

Probably shouldn't have said that. As if he'd make himself at home. The man was a professional. And he had the blank face and hard eyes look straight back in business this morning. Which was right and good. Just because you spent the night in my room (not bed) didn't mean there would be any change in our professional relationship or business arrangement. I needed to get this man's position in my life straight and stop overthinking everything. The bodyguard was making me a neurotic wreck.

Coffee would fix everything. Then time for some more unpacking and a little work.

I reached for the mug, overshot, and knocked it straight off the counter. It crashed at my feet, splattering hot liquid everywhere.

"Shit."

Down the hall, the bathroom door dramatically flew open. Next Ziggy stepped out with a gun in one hand. The other hand, meanwhile, kept the towel around his waist held together. So. Much. Skin. Like seriously.

His assessing eyes immediately took in the scene. "Are you okay, Miss Cooper?"

"Yeah. I just…um."

My brain basically melted. Holy hell he was ripped. Long, lean, and built in all the ways. I mean, his suit hinted at it, but it was a little startling to see how fit the man actually was. Bet he could snap me in half with one hand. Though he'd also look delightful with a dad or a bear bod. The man carried himself so well. Also, I just enjoyed looking at him that much. Which (again) was wrong. Were I not a lapsed Catholic, I'd have been doing Hail Marys for days, thanks to the lustful thoughts this man inspired.

What was wrong with me?

I needed a moment to pull myself together, and I closed my eyes. Yes, much better. Without all of his hotness in my face my brain could actually function. "I'm fine. Just clumsy."

"Your skin is red," he commented.

"Oh, I'm blushing? That's because it's embarrassing being such a klutz," my lying tongue lied.

"No, your foot."

Then came a soft clink amongst other muted sounds. A cloth dabbed carefully at my foot. I opened my eyelids to see what was happening. Ziggy Thayer was on bended knee in front of me. His dark hair, wide shoulders, and even the long line of his spine were on display. With tea towel in hand, he wiped the hot coffee off my skin.

"I don't think you're burnt." He gazed up at me with those oh so serious eyes. He had beautiful olive skin with a couple of white scars on his back. "Does it feel okay?"

"It feels...good. I mean fine. Yeah. No worries."

"Lift your foot for me."

"My foot?"

"That's right." He waited patiently until I did as asked. Once I had one raised a little off the ground, he gripped my ankle carefully with one hand, wiping the drops of coffee off my skin with the other. His hand was warm, the pads of his fingers slightly rough. Once done, he tapped lightly on the toes of my other foot to signal it was up and repeated the procedure.

All I could do was stare. He did the job with such care, so gentle yet thorough. The man made my skin tingle, especially my crotch. Even my boyfriend from a few years back with the mild foot fetish had never turned me on this much. Did the bodyguard even know the effect he had on me? The outline of my nipples through the thin material of my shirt certainly didn't qualify as coy. Sheesh. Clients throwing themselves at him probably happened all of the time. After all, his job description basically involved turning up and taking charge at the precise moment someone was at their most vulnerable. And being super-buff, apparently. Recipe for lust. Didn't mean I needed to be crass or improper.

"Thank you for that, Ziggy. Much appreciated."

"Take a step back and I'll clean up the broken pieces so you don't cut yourself."

"You're not my housekeeper," I said. "You don't have to do that."

Again, he just waited until I complied. It was so strange, having him tend to me, having someone look after me like this. Carefully, he proceeded to gather up all of the broken pieces and place them in the tea towel. When he rose to his feet, towering over me, I searched his face for something. Some hint of emotion. I found nothing, though it seemed there was heat radiating from his skin. Either that or I was blushing again. Damn inconvenient habit.

"I'll take that," I said. "Thanks again."

He nodded and gave me the damp package before heading back to the bathroom without another word. And I stood there like an idiot all dazed and confused, watching him go. As if I could do anything else with him walking around my apartment half naked.

Perhaps I should take Lena up on her offer of a blind date. I might need to give it more thought. Who knows, maybe a man even more divine than Ziggy was out there right now, waiting for me. Someone who didn't come with pesky concerns for professional cordiality. In the meantime, cleaning up the rest of the spillage and a nice cold shower seemed like a great idea.

"He gave the box along with five dollars to one of the regular delivery guys as he was walking inside," she said.

Ziggy, Sarah from reception, and I stood gathered around the reception desk. Another bland brown box sat there with a label bearing my name. She'd called up no more than five minutes before, asking if we were available to come down. And it wasn't so she could deliver good news.

"We got him on the security cameras, but he was wearing all black clothing and a motorcycle helmet," continued Sarah. "No distinguishing features that I could see."

I peeled back the packing tape. "We need to make sure."

"Detective Ortega will be over in an hour or so," said Ziggy, sliding his cell back into his pocket. "Are you sure you don't want to wait?"

"Just in case. She's a busy woman, I don't want to waste her time."

"At least let me open it."

"I can do it. I'll be fine. It's my mess, after all."

He didn't look happy, but he didn't stop me. He just hovered next to me, close by, and I could almost feel his muscles quivering like a sprinter at the starting gate, ready to react. Nobody said anything as I carefully pried open the cardboard box. It felt like there were ants crawling over my skin. Someone walking over my grave, maybe. Because sure enough, stinky rust brown-stained material lay folded inside. My stomach twisted and turned. A shriveled piece of raw meat sat amongst it all. Another heart, perhaps? Whatever it was, it was disgusting. Deranged.

"That's enough, Miss Cooper," said Ziggy. "Please step away. We've established it's either from him or a copycat."

"I can see some of the label on the material. It's a piece from my lingerie line." As asked, I took a step back, arms wrapped around myself. "So much for hoping he'd lost interest."

Ziggy looked up. "The detective will want to talk to the delivery guy."

"He couldn't wait, but I've got his number and the five-dollar bill," said Sarah.

"Good." He turned to me. "Are you all right? Miss Cooper? Mae?"

"Hmm? Yeah." I shrugged. "The tissue paper he wrapped it in, it's kind of an orange color, isn't it? Same as the last one, I think."

"Hard to tell with all the blood. You positive you're okay, not feeling nauseous or faint?"

"No, I'm fine. Basically." I sighed. "I'm not some swooning maiden and there's not much I can do about this that we're not doing already, is there? They sure must hate me, whoever they are. He even bought it in my size."

"Did he?" Ziggy's fingers twitched at his side. As if he might have liked to punch something, or I don't know what. But I could have used a hand to hold on to right about then.

"What's up?" asked a deep voice.

In walked David Ferris with his arm slung around his wife Evelyn Ferris's neck. Judging from the collection of shopping bags in his spare hand, they'd been out and about supporting the neighborhood businesses. They were a pretty hot looking couple, him with his dark hair and tattoos and her all blonde and curvy. I'd met a fair number of famous and important people over the years but they were impressive in their low-key rock'n'roll royalty cool way. Despite the sucky situation, Mom would be impressed when I told her. She was a big Stage Dive fan.

"Oh no," said Evelyn. "They didn't send something else?"

Ziggy stood straight and tall, even more on duty than before, if possible. "I'm afraid so."

"We haven't been properly introduced yet." She held out her hand to me for shaking. "I'm Evelyn and this is my husband, David. I've been hoping we'd cross paths. Lena's told me a lot about you."

I managed a smile despite the weird feeling in the pit of my stomach. "I'm Mae. Hi."

They both shook my hand, casting a couple of worried glances at the latest dreaded box of horrors. Sarah got back behind the reception desk and with a pair of plastic gloves on her hands, carried the box out back, out of sight. Can't say I was sorry to see it go. Meanwhile, Ziggy and David gave each other the standard dude tipping chins in a manly fashion greeting. Guess they'd worked together a lot. Though Ziggy didn't seem particularly relaxed around the couple. But then, it would be a professional relationship. Like what he had with me.

"We're being watched," said Ev, looking over her shoulder out the wide glass windows beside the front door. "Photographer across the street."

David frowned. "Might be best to head upstairs."

"Guess the paparazzi will be back in force when they hear about this." I balled my hands up into fists. All of the old sensations of feeling powerless in this shitty situation swamped me. Yay for self-pity. And by yay, I mean boo.

"Listen." She moved closer. "We're having some friends over tonight and we'd love you to join us. Hopefully get your mind off all of this for a few hours. Say around eight?"

"That's sweet of you, but I'm not sure I'm in the mood."

"No, she's right. You should come," said David. "You'll bring her, yeah, Ziggy?"

Ziggy just turned to me. "It'll be safe," he said.

Talk about being put on the spot. Best to give in with good grace. It wasn't like I'd be doing anything else, apart from moping at home. Go, party girl me. "Sure. Why not? Thank you."

CHAPTER FIVE

"Okay. I think I'm about ready."

Ziggy looked up from where he sat on the couch with his cell in hand. And he just kind of stared.

"What?"

He swallowed.

"Ziggy?"

Still no response. Huh.

My Emporio Armani sleeveless white silk blouse with a cute asymmetric fold neckline, dark blue jeans, and Louboutin leopard print patent leather pumps with four-inch heels delighted me no end. I also wore diamond solitaire stud earrings and a Cartier diamond and stainless steel bracelet watch. My long dark hair was styled into a slick ponytail and glossy red lips and I was good to go wow some rock stars. Or at least make a solid attempt at keeping up with them and their wives. But I couldn't tell what my bodyguard thought.

He slowly rose to his feet, gaze still stuck on me.

"Are you going to say something?" I asked.

"This what normally happens when you spend two hours in the bathroom?" His voice seemed rougher than normal. Also, this was another distinct break in the usual professional protocol. And I relished it even more than I did getting my greedy hands early on the new season's heels and matching clutch. Another industry perk. "Sorry, miss. I shouldn't have said that."

I laughed. "You haven't seen me done up before, have you? This is me as Mae Cooper, model. Pleased to meet you."

He didn't smile, but little crinkles appeared beside his eyes. Guess it was close enough.

"I don't even look like her without a few hours' worth of hair and makeup," I said with a smile. "Much better than regular old Mae who slums around in old T-shirts with her hair in a messy bun, huh?"

"I wouldn't say that."

"No?"

"No." And he said nothing more. All of the gorgeous angles of his face stayed in their typical no-emotion setting. Lady Gaga should have just dedicated the song "Poker Face" to him and been done with it.

After Detective Ortega's visit a few hours ago, it had been nice to have the distraction of a get together to look forward to. Given that the stalker creep had worn gloves, and given them no leads, there wasn't much they could do. Plus, she probably had way more serious crimes to investigate than me and my unwelcome deliveries. No point dwelling on the situation. I was committed to putting it out of my head. Or at least trying.

"Well, all right then," I said. "Let's go."

Half a dozen people were already hanging out in David and Ev's apartment. It was basically the same layout as mine, but here the floor boards were painted black, and there were lime green couches. Lou Reed played on the stereo, gold and platinum records lined the hallways, and a plentiful collection of amps and guitars sat on display in one corner. Thankfully, Lena and Jimmy were in attendance so at least I knew them.

"I could have been a model," announced Mal Ericson, the drummer for Stage Dive. He sat on the sofa beside his heavily pregnant wife Anne. "Supermodel, I mean. Obviously."

David just snorted in disbelief.

"Yeah?" I asked, being polite.

"Absolutely. I can strike a pose." Mal jumped to his feet, doing his best duck lips. "Just watch."

"So perfect," said Lena, tongue in cheek. "That's exactly how they do it. Good job, Mal."

Anne just shook her head. "Please don't encourage him."

"I'm a natural." Mal ran through a variety of awkward looking poses that would have put a yoga instructor to the test. Madonna in her *Vogue* heyday would not have been jealous of his styling. I daresay, Madonna would have laughed her tight buns off. "When you think about it, it seems almost cruel to deny the world my beauty. Hidden at the back of a stage behind a kit is just a waste."

"I was just thinking that," said Lena, taking a sip of white wine.

"Who's hidden away?" complained David. "The platform you mount the drums on is almost a podium, you're up so high. I swear it gets half a foot higher with every tour, you show pony."

"That's only because you guys wouldn't let me play suspended in a cage above the crowd, Mötley Crüe style."

"I'm down with any plan that puts the words 'Mal' and 'cage' in the same sentence," said Jimmy, the lead singer. "Besides, I've been on about a million photo shoots with you, Mal. Standing still basically kills you. How the hell do you think you have the attention span to actually model?"

"I'm dynamic. Constantly in motion. It's part of my look. Check it out, this is my blue steel," yelled Mal, rushing into the hallway to do a handstand. Upside down, he asked, "Great. Right, Mae? So unexpected. Avant garde even."

Oh my God. "Um, yeah. So great. There are no words to describe it really."

He proceeded to walk around on his hands clown style, his long blond hair looking ridiculous as it almost brushed the floor. "You have Anna Wintour's number, right? Get her on the horn, I'm ready for the cover of *Vogue*."

"I will definitely get right on that in just a moment or two."

Lena huffed out a laugh.

"I'm kind of surprised you even know who Anna Wintour is," said Ev, beer in hand. She stood beside the end of the long couch with David next to her. His arm hung loose around her waist.

All these happy couples. *insert gagging noises here* No, I shouldn't be so down on love. Love was great. It just hadn't worked out for me in recent years. Or like…ever.

"Why?" Mal righted himself. "I'll have you know I'm very fashionable. I know things. Tell them, Mae."

"Apparently he knows things," I dutifully repeated.

"Babe, those are the same pair of ripped black jeans you've been wearing since I met you," said Anne. "You still wear band shirts with holes in them the size of my head, that you've owned since you were like twelve."

"So? They're classics. Vintage. All the cool kids are wearing them."

"Anne, maybe don't leave him alone with the baby for the first eighteen years or so," suggested Ev. "Just in case."

"Sounds sensible," mumbled Anne.

From the other side of the room, standing against the wall, Ziggy gave me a small shake of his head at the drummer's antics.

I suggested Ziggy take the night off since I wasn't leaving the building, and he'd already admitted I'd be safe surrounded by the Stage Dive crew and all. Never really occurred to me how full-on the role of bodyguard actually was. This would have been the perfect opportunity for him to catch up with his own life et cetera. But he'd declined. Apparently the man took his job seriously and was determined to be stuck to me like glue during all hours of the day. I can't say I didn't like having him around. Well, I could, but I'd be lying.

I grabbed an olive from the charcuterie board on the low coffee table. It had salami, prosciutto, nuts, cheeses, dried fruits, crackers, pretzels, breadsticks, decorative edible flowers, and everything else under the sun. I could have fed my face the entire yummy thing. Nearby bottles of wine and beer sat in ice-filled buckets. These people knew how to party in style. No question, I liked my new neighbors. Even Mal had a certain charm. In fact, his craziness was almost relaxing. There was no need to fumble for conversation topics or anything around him. You could just sit back and enjoy the show.

"We're here!" called out a low voice from the front door.

In trooped the band's bass player, Ben Nicholson, followed by a whole bunch of people.

"Mae," said Lena. "Meet Ben and his wife, Lizzy. Next comes our baby star boy solo act himself, Adam Dillon."

"Wish you wouldn't call me that," said Adam, a handsome slouchy rock'n'roll looking dude in his mid-twenties. Lots of hair and tattoos. Very cool. I'd certainly heard of him—his music was all over the radio and music TV channels these days.

"Wish on, my sweet." Lena smiled. "Martha, his manager, and of course, Sam, her fiancé and the owner of the security company we're all loving and using."

The beefy-looking bald man gave me a nod. "Miss Cooper. Pleasure to meet you in person."

I raised a hand in welcome. "Call me Mae, please. Nice to meet you too."

"I trust Ziggy's been looking after you." He tipped his chin in the direction of my bodyguard, who gave a brief nod in return.

"He's been great, thank you."

"Where did you get those?" Martha, a svelte brunette, stared at my heels. "I've had them on pre-order forever."

"They were a gift," I said, holding up the matching clutch.

"Ugh. I hate you." She winked. "I need a drink."

"Your wish is my command." Sam poured her a glass of champagne. "I thought it all went rather well."

"The show was a huge success, but the open bar was crap. They didn't even put anything decent in Adam's dressing room for me to steal."

"It was for charity and it was great exposure," said Ben, taking a seat on the couch and pulling his wife down onto his lap.

"Which is why I booked it. But now I need to chill and drink Ev's Dom Pérignon."

Ev smiled. "That's why I bought it for you."

"Bon, you're off now. Time to relax and have a drink." Sam handed a beer to the last man to wander into the room.

He was tall and built along the same lines as Ziggy. In fact, come to think of it, they looked a hell of a lot alike. He too wore a dark suit, expertly tailored. After accepting his drink with a nod, he went to stand beside Ziggy against the wall. At the party, but not really a part of it.

"So, I had a new idea for the nursery," said Martha, champagne in hand. "What about a black and white plaid feature wall?"

"Plaid?" asked Anne, hands smoothing over her big belly. "Hmm. Interesting."

Lizzy frowned. "Have I got my dates wrong? Or isn't this baby due like next week or so?"

Anne calmly nodded.

"Nursery's finished," said Mal. "After months of debate, you two finally decided on a buttercup yellow with Boho-Farmhouse accents. Whatever that all means."

"And it's beautiful. But it doesn't mean we can't fine tune it," said Martha.

"Still planning on a natural delivery?" asked Lizzy.

"Absolutely." Mal nodded. "I've been reading about it. What's best for the baby is best for the momma."

Anne cleared her throat. "Hey. Excuse me. This momma will have whatever drugs she feels necessary to push a baby out of her vagina and she isn't waiting for your permission."

He hung his head. "Yes, pumpkin. Whatever you say."

Face turned away, David quietly laughed.

"Oh yeah, you think it's funny now," hissed Mal. "But just wait until it's your turn to deal with psycho pregnancy hormones, man. Then we'll see who's laughing."

Jimmy nodded, all wise-like. "He's actually speaking the truth for once. This one time, Lena burst into tears and threw a spoon at me because I'd finished the last of the chocolate fudge ice cream. Then she made me go out and get some more. It was three in the morning. I had a red mark on my forehead for days."

"I apologized for that," said Lena. "I can't throw for the life of me. How was I to know I'd actually manage to hit you?"

"When you're half asleep it's hard to duck in time when shit comes flying at your head."

"Poor baby." Lena drew him in, kissing his furrowed brow.

"Lizzy cried every time she saw a show or a TV ad with an animal or family in it," added Ben, the big, bearded dude. "Made watching anything impossible."

The blonde in his lap scowled. "I had feelings. Deal with it. We can't all be stalwart and repressed, Benjamin."

Ben just raised his brows. Men. So stupid.

Over by the wall, Ziggy, Sam, and Bon were chatting. On the couch, Ben and David started talking about a new producer they wanted to work with. Which left Lena making weird noises in my direction for some reason.

"Pssst. Mae, I need to speak to you in the bathroom."

"Um, okay." I set aside my drink and followed her into the hallway. We didn't even make it into the bathroom before she turned on me in the doorway. Heads together, she grabbed my shoulders to ensure I had no chance of escape. Nope. I was trapped. "What are we doing?"

"We're talking."

"About?"

Her glossy red lips curled into a grin. "What do you think of Adam?"

"Well, I'm sure he's a very nice young man," I said. "And he makes great music. I was jogging to his album just the other day."

"Mae, get with the program. I mean as in you and him dating. Duh." She flicked her hair.

"Don't you flick your hair at me, young lady."

"I will when you're being deliberately obtuse."

"Oh my God. You haven't talked to him about me, have you?" I sighed. "Lena. Please. Tell me this isn't a setup."

"Of course it's not a setup. Relax."

"Phew."

"So…" She waited not so patiently.

"Forget it. I'm done with fuck boys, no matter how seemingly nice, pretty, or talented they may be."

"He's not a fuck boy…exactly. He's just young."

"Yeah. That's kind of my point."

Now it was her turn to sigh. And she did so heavily. There was even some impressive heaving of breasts. "You know, you're going to have to get over your idiot ex eventually."

"I am over him. But there were lessons to be learned there." I leaned forward and smacked a kiss upon her cheek. "Thank you, but I don't want to date your younger, exciting rock'n'roll dude. My next boyfriend will be someone loyal and dependable, staid and ever so slightly safe and boring."

She just wrinkled her nose.

"My dream man will be home every night in time for dinner. Isn't even on any social media. He'll enjoy such pursuits as stamp collecting, bird spotting, and macramé."

"Woo. Party time," she said flatly. "Sounds like we'll be checking him for signs of life."

"Right? It'll be great." I smiled. "Plus he will be totally a hundred-and-ten-percent into me. Think I'm a mighty and benevolent goddess, worship the ground I walk on. That sort of thing."

"You do know it's possible to find a decent man who thinks you're a queen, but doesn't bore you to sleep, right?"

"Eh. Why risk it? Besides, I could do with more beauty sleep. Sleep is under-rated." I neglected to mention how a certain someone had managed to successfully get me off to sleep just yesterday. But Ziggy definitely wouldn't fit my new monotonous requirement for all future boyfriends. Not a chance.

"When it all goes to hell and you eventually come to your senses, don't say I didn't try to rescue you from a life of tedium, crafts, outdoor activities, and bad sex," said Lena with a pout. She had a great pout. Almost as good as mine.

"And quiet adoration. Don't forget the quiet adoration."

With a huff of disgust, she marched back into the main room. And in doing so, walked straight past Ziggy and Bon. Two bodyguards who were more than close enough to have heard every last word we'd just said. In fact, Ziggy was now staring straight at me. Shit.

"Hi." I raised a hand. "Having a nice time?"

"Yes, miss."

"Great."

The big man standing next to him cleared his throat.

"Miss Cooper, let me to introduce my brother to you," said Ziggy, pulling on the cuff of his shirt. A nervous habit, perhaps? I don't know.

Bon stepped forward with his hand out, every bit as tall, dark, and handsome as his brother. But with a hint of the devil in his smile. "Pleasure to meet you, ma'am. I'm a big fan of your work."

"Thank you. Are you a bodyguard too?"

"I am," he said and there was something in his tone. "I was hoping I'd get the chance to work with you, but Ziggy tells me he has it covered."

"Ziggy has been great."

Bon slapped his brother on the back so hard Ziggy winced. What the hell was going on here? Sibling rivalry or something? As an only child, families with more than one kid kind of fascinated me. I looked like Mom so it wasn't about having someone I resembled. But I'd never had anyone around my own age to bicker about the silly everyday stuff or to lean on when times were tough. Someone who grew up with me and came from the same background. Not that I suffered. Mom and Gran are and were my bedrock. But it would have been nice to have a brother or sister.

"I'm sure you both get asked this all the time, but I take it your parents were big music fans?" I asked.

Ziggy nodded. "Mom's a rock chick from way back. Bowie and AC/DC are her favorites."

"We were pretty much raised on that music," said Bon. "And hey, at least there weren't five other kids in the class with the same name."

"True enough. And years later, here you both are, surrounded by rock'and'roll."

Ziggy opened his mouth to speak, but Bon got in first: "Yeah, but not in the way Mom was hoping. She was trying to bring up a couple of boys who could wield axes in the musical sense."

"I see. Not axes in the actual sense, like you two."

"Exactly."

"Except by axes he means guns," said Ziggy.

I nodded. "Gotcha."

Bon gave me another warm smile while Ziggy frowned at his brother. Interesting. This conversation had the air of a territorial pissing competition. Only it was hard to figure out if it was due to competitive business stuff, general sibling rivalry, or what. His brother sure could make him react, however.

"Not to kill the mood," said Bon, "but I'm sorry to hear about your situation. There are some assholes out there."

"Language," hissed his brother.

"It's fine." I looked away for a moment. "And yes, there are."

"Glad my brother's got your back through this trying time. You couldn't ask for anyone more capable." At this, he gave said brother another of those evil back slaps.

"Thanks," said Ziggy, somewhat drily.

"Though if he ever needs a day off, I'd be happy to step in and watch you, Miss Cooper."

Ziggy's jaw firmed. "She doesn't need you watching her."

"Just offering."

"You're being unprofessional."

"How am I being unprofessional, ensuring that our client's needs are being met?"

"Thanks anyway, brother. You've got enough on your plate. Luke or Adelaide can cover if necessary." If Ziggy's eyes had shot out laser beams, I would not have been surprised. Well, I would have, but not by much. This interaction was nothing less than fascinating.

"There's a female bodyguard on staff?" I asked.

"She's busy." And that was it. That was all Ziggy said. He and his big blank handsome face.

Shit. "Oh, no. I didn't mean to imply…you're doing a wonderful job. There's no need to bring anyone else in."

Bon smirked, but tried to hide it. That was about enough for me.

"Lovely to meet you," I said.

Ziggy nodded. "Miss."

"Miss Cooper," his brother added.

I got my butt back to the couch and retrieved my drink. But I could feel his eyes on me. All damn night, Ziggy continued to watch.

CHAPTER SIX

"Nice bodyguard."

I frowned. "Why is everyone always commenting on my bodyguard?"

"Because he's hot," said Abigael, the hair stylist and make-up artist.

"Yeah, but we're around hot people all the time. It's basically kind of the point of our industry."

At this, the petite blonde stopped and pondered.

The man himself stood at the other end of the large room, out of the way near the coffee and pastries table. Not that he was indulging. I'd have to steal an extra almond croissant to eat later to make up for his lack of pastry love. Once more, his face seemed set in stone. His big body remained still while his gaze constantly wandered the area. We hadn't talked much on the drive over to the studio, even though it was on the other side of town. After last night's weirdness with his brother, and the renewed attention of the paparazzi, and more lack of sleep, I didn't feel like chatting. Truth was, the man set me on edge. This entire situation set me on edge. And today, I needed to focus on work.

So I'd guzzled caffeine while Abigael fixed the bags and dark shadows beneath my eyes with eye masks and various other tricks. Lucky for me, the woman was magic with a messy face. She'd spent years living in Los Angeles fixing party people the day after, getting them ready to face the world and the camera. Her skills were legendary.

"I think it's all the big dick energy he's giving off," she finally announced.

"Huh."

"Now stop talking. Lip gloss touch-up and you're good to go."

I sat in the make-up chair clad in a long white robe. My hair was a dark silky fall straight down my back to my bra strap. My eyes were smoky and my lips were red. A nice sexy look.

Abigael finished and stepped back with a happy smile. "You're my masterpiece."

"You say that to everyone you work on."

"Yeah, but I mean it this time. Damn, I'm good."

I laughed.

Abigael was great to work with. She always had a funny story about a bridezilla or similar to spill during the hour or more I spent in the chair. She touched up the lip gloss then fixed a few spots where my skin had either reddened or darkened.

"Stop frowning," she mumbled. "Not that I don't blame you with the stuff going on right now."

"You've been on the gossip sites, huh?"

"Didn't need to. It's the talk of the town."

I groaned. "Slow news week. This too shall pass."

"Sorry," she said. "You probably don't want to talk about it. My bad."

"No, it's fine." I stretched my neck when she stopped touching up my face with concealer for a moment. "There's a lot going on right now. Kind of hard not to think about it. I tried to keep it quiet, but that clearly didn't work. All of last night I just lay awake trying to figure out who it could be."

"So what do you know about him?"

I took a deep breath, thinking it through. "He knows my proper address. Not too difficult to find out, but means he's not an amateur sending stuff care of my agent. Mind you, is there even such a thing as an amateur stalker?"

"Good question."

"And he knows stuff about me. The lingerie was my label and the right size. He also has access to cow hearts, though probably he could just have got them from the butcher."

"Blech."

"Right?" I shivered. "He's clever and opportunistic, handing stuff off to the delivery guy and paying him to bring it in. But at the same time, him coming to the building again shows he's willing to take some risks. There were a few ways that little stunt might not have worked out."

Abigael just frowned. It was a frowning kind of topic of discussion.

"He's bloodthirsty, obviously. Likes using a knife."

"You're freaking me out," said Abi. "This is why I don't watch murder documentaries."

"Imagine being in my shoes. It's always at the back of my mind, making me jumpy as a cat on a hot tin roof as Elizabeth Taylor would say."

Abi gave me a small smile. It was a shitty situation. No hiding that. She finished up my face while Lena stood in front of the shooting area with its all-white surrounds. This room had no windows to let in outside light. She had another room upstairs with large industrial style windows that was cool to work with. Air-conditioners were doing their best, but I still felt the heat from the lights. I blinked a few times, adjusting to the fake eyelashes and the brightness.

"I like this look." Zane, my co-designer for the lingerie line, took my robe. "The demi-cup bra was a nice idea. Goes well with the boy shorts."

"We work magic together, dude."

Zane sniffed. "Don't call me dude. Dude."

I held back a smile. "You were right, the trompe l'oeil embroidery is beautiful in light blue. And I like the opaque back on the panties."

"Such a sweet set. You look almost virginal," sighed Lena, lifting her camera to her face.

"Oh, I'm afraid those days are long gone, sweetie," said Zane with a smile.

"Nice. Very nice." I mock frowned. "You people are supposed to be my friends."

"Please. Fashion means never having friends. Now stand there and look pretty."

Lizzo played loud and proud over the stereo, setting the mood. I could only make out the shadow of Ziggy's face due to all the lighting and him standing near the back of the room. But then he stepped forward far enough for me to see him and holy shit. The look in his dark eyes made me catch my breath.

And I definitely wasn't imagining the I want to eat you from top to toe looks. Not even a little.

Though, now that I thought about it, he'd liked the look of me all made up for the party last night. With Abigael the wonder make-up artist having worked me over and the addition of some amazing scanty lingerie, odds were, a heterosexual male (of which I was pretty certain he was one) in this particular situation would like me even more. That's all it was. Probably. Anyway, points to me for cracking his professional façade.

"Whatever you're thinking about, please keep thinking about it." Lena busily worked her camera, clicking off shot after shot. "The lusty dreamy look on your face is freaking perfect."

"Agreed," said Zane.

Suddenly, I felt exposed in a way that had nothing to do with standing there in my underwear. But what could I do? Fuck hiding. I wasn't going to try and make myself small for anyone. I was Mae Cooper, goddammit. And if I was into a dude, then so be it, that dude was one damn lucky man. Though it might have been simpler had he not been standing right there staring at me while I worked. Oh well. Such is life. Lena gave me more instructions and I did my job.

The next piece was a risqué though slightly less revealing lace trim chemise in fire engine red. Abigael put my hair back into a messy ponytail for the piece. Same as before, Ziggy neither stepped back into the shadows nor took his gaze off me. I felt very protected. And ever so slightly turned on. A sensation I didn't tend to experience at shoots generally speaking. You might flirt and play a little, but it never went beyond that. For me at least. However, Ziggy and his heated looks were driving me straight over the edge. A problem since damp panties in the current situation would be not only wrong but distressingly obvious.

Unfortunately, after the chemise came a beautiful black semi-sheer plunging demi-bralette with a lace thong. My breasts were barely contained, let alone my behind. One deep breath and there'd be flesh in everyone's faces. With the thong also came a super embarrassing though not uncommon in this industry moment. Having a zit on your butt covered with concealer in front of a bunch of people wasn't so great. But these things tended to happen with skimpy swimwear or ladies' intimate apparel. Such was life. I tried to stay professional about it and crack my usual jokes. Emphasis on tried. At least there was a bathroom/changing room for the actual switching of outfits. Ziggy was probably seeing enough of my tits and ass for one day. More might get seriously awkward.

"We have a rather pointed and prominent nipple situation," announced Zane at around this point. And here came more awkward. "Very pretty, Mae. But for this shoot we need to keep the focus on the fashion. Abi, you got the stickers?"

My day was just going from strength to strength. "Tell the truth, Zane. You're just jealous you don't get to shove your nipples in people's faces on a regular basis."

"Actually, you have a point." He grinned. "I bet I'd be amazing at it. Give you a run for your money."

I laughed.

Next came the white balconette bodysuit with embroidery on the cups I'd affectionately named "bang the bride." My hair had been styled into a fancy windblown up-do. We liked to mix up the looks, keep things interesting. Subtly change the story being told in each picture. Ziggy's expression this time around was especially gratifying. His cheekbones stood out in stark relief, his jaw fixed. The man just stared. And he made it next to impossible to keep my eyes off of him, let alone to not think about hot sex. With him, explicitly.

For certain, he had to be reacting to the ultra-glamorous model Mae Cooper. Not the boring old clumsy forgetful real me who wanted to be loved. Didn't need the attention, but I sure did want it. I had to keep reminding myself of this oh so salient fact when it came to Ziggy's attentions. Protecting my heart in this situation was the wise thing to do.

You'd think a model would have better self-esteem, but my current hang-ups came from an unfortunate reality. The ex hadn't even liked me taking off my makeup. Said it made me look so much prettier. I know, I know. I should have shot him in the crotch rather than deal with his bullshit. Changing my Netflix account password after we broke up was a pretty glorious feeling, I'll tell you. I timed it for the day the new season of his favorite show came out. With a bit of luck he was two episodes in when the universe came crashing down around him. Serves him right. He'd always been cheap with the exception of the stupendously stupid flowers he'd so recently sent. Just because he earned millions didn't make him any less of an ass.

But back to the topic at hand, the last thing I needed would be to accidentally deliberately fall straight back into bed with someone who got real me and fake me mixed up. Then there was the part where Ziggy currently worked for me and all. I was sort of his boss. It wouldn't be right for all sorts of responsible adult reasons for me to take him up on the surprisingly heated looks he was throwing my way today.

Stupid hormones and thoughts and feelings. Why did we even need them? All they ever did was cause trouble. Me and my vibrator definitely had a hot date lined up for tonight. First, however, maybe I should give Sam a call and suggest Ziggy needed a day off. I know I did. A little distance right now might be wise. Get his hotness out of my face for a while.

Lena finally lowered her camera. "You were on fire today."

"Thanks." This made sense what with the excessive heat happening in my panties and all.

"We are going to sell some lingerie, I tell you!"

"Good to hear." I smiled, taking my robe back from Zane.

It'd been a long and confusing day. Though the mental aerobics pondering Ziggy and his behavior sure did wonders for taking my mind off the horrible deliveries and evil stalker person. That mess had hardly crossed my mind at all.

I got dressed back into my black tank top, skinny jeans, strappy sandals, and big sunglasses. With the fancy hair and full make-up, if the paparazzi were still hanging around, which they inevitably would be given my luck, they'd have pretty glam shots without the need for me dressing up. Not that this was the kind of publicity I needed nor required, but I suppose it would make a change from them snapping me with my baggy eyes and shoddy clothes over the last week. That was something, at least.

There were hugs and air kisses aplenty as we finished up. Lena's studio was in a gated area so the paparazzi were sort of milling around out beyond the gates. You'd want to be patient. Sometimes I really felt for them. It must be such a boring job, standing around for long stretches of time. Of course, you'd also want to be a bit of an invasive jerk who didn't particularly care about people's privacy during their times of trouble.

The sun sat low in the sky and the fresh air outside was a welcome change after all the hours of being cooped up inside. It would be nice not to be touched for a while too. Most everyone on the many shoots I'd been on had been professional and matter of fact, but getting your personal space back at the end of a shoot was a nice sensation.

It wasn't far to the Rover. Ziggy strode slightly to the side and slightly in front of me. Guess the position kept me in the edge of his field of vision. We still weren't really talking much today, though the mood felt thick for want of a better word. Or off, maybe?

I don't know where the stranger had been hiding. In between the parked cars, maybe. But all of a sudden he was barreling toward me. He was thin, but tall, wearing a baggy T-shirt, chinos, and a faded baseball cap pulled down low.

In an instant, Ziggy was there, quickly side stepping. He placed himself between us.

"I just..." the man started.

"Step back," said Ziggy, hands out in front, ready to hold this guy back. "Move away."

"What's your reaction to the gruesome parcels delivered to your apartment, Mae?" he pressed on, running straight into Ziggy's hands. It didn't seem to faze him at all. "Have the police got any suspects?"

Over at the gate, the paparazzi were going nuts taking pictures of the altercation. I tried to keep my face down, but the jerk just kept shouting questions at me. His voice was so loud and demanding it was jarring. And the colors on his cap were weirdly familiar. Faded, but familiar.

"You're trespassing. You need to leave." Ziggy walked the man back a step. Then he reached into his pocket and used the key fob to unlock the car. "Miss Cooper, get into the car, please."

No wonder the colors were familiar, they were from my ex's football team. Orange and blue. And the tissue paper in the boxes had been a kind of orange color too. Neither Ziggy nor the detective had wanted to commit given the bloody state of the paper, but I was certain. The man pushed forward, ramming Ziggy with his elbow. "I just want to talk to her."

"Who are you?" I snapped. Plenty of journalists had wanted to talk to me over the years. But this level of animosity was something new. "Who do you work for?"

Lip curled, he sneered, "Come on, Mae, have a heart."

All of a sudden, one hell of a bad feeling hit me. My stomach sunk through the ground. "You're him. Oh my God. You sent those things. The hearts and..."

His face turned manic, the whites of his eyes huge.

"Ziggy, be careful," I yelled. "It's him."

Immediately, the man upped his attempts to get at me. He and Ziggy tussled and fought. Then Ziggy grunted as there was a flash of metal. A blade was held aloft, clasped in the maniac's hand, Ziggy's fingers hard around his wrist. The whole scene was horrible and scary and happening so fast. With great force, Ziggy slammed his forehead into the other man's face. Bone crunched and the man howled in pain. So much damn blood. It gushed out of his nose, covering his lips and chin. Next Ziggy smashed his knee into the man's groin and he dropped toward the ground in an almighty rush.

Through it all, Ziggy had kept a stranglehold on the arm holding the knife. As the guy dropped, Ziggy grabbed his wrist with both hands, spun around and snapped the arm downwards. There was a crack as the man's elbow met Ziggy's shoulder and was forced into bending in the wrong direction. The knife clattered to the ground. Within a flash, Ziggy was on him. Now the guy's wrist was bent in another way again, locked in between Ziggy's legs and twisted around and down in an ugly manner. Ziggy pulled the hand inward and upward, making the guy's full weight all hang from the back of his wrist. He screamed.

Ziggy nodded and relaxed his grip. "Sit," he growled. "And if you ever want to use this wrist again in your lifetime, do not move so much as an inch."

The man just moaned, curling on himself, his free hand trying to reach down to his damaged balls. It was over. Holy cow.

Meanwhile, I felt cold and weird for some reason. My heart hammered inside my chest and my knees turned to water. From the violence, maybe? Whatever. I didn't have time for this. I had to do something to help. Paparazzi over at the gates shouted out questions and pushed and strained to get the best shot, but we all just ignored them. The whole situation seemed surreal. Like something out of a bad movie.

"Mae," said Ziggy, looking up at me from his weird position atop the stalker. He actually looked weirdly relaxed, like he could sit there all day like that. "You did good, figuring it out. It's okay now. Situation's under control. Can you hear me?"

"Ah. Y-yes."

"I need you."

"You do? All right. What do I do?"

"You have to make some phone calls, okay? Can you do that for me, please, while I keep an eye on this piece of shit?"

"Sure." I set my handbag on the ground, kneeling beside it. So much stuff. But my cell was definitely in here somewhere. "Right."

Ziggy scowled. He took one hand off the wrist lock he had the guy in, and wiped it on his jacket in annoyance. It was slick with blood. Dripping with it. No sooner had he wiped his fingers off than thick red streams of blood coursed back down it.

My jaw fell open. "You're bleeding. He cut you."

"First rule of a knife fight. Someone's gonna bleed." Resigning himself to the fact that the hand wasn't going to miraculously stop with the blood, he raised the arm up and pinned it between his neck and shoulder. Compression and elevation, I guess. His gaze returned to the moaning man beneath him. "I'm fine. Find your cell. Knowing your bag, if you start looking now it should only take an hour or two."

"That's not funny," I snapped. "I'll call an ambulance after I make whatever call you want me to make. The police first, right?"

"Police first. And I don't need an ambulance. I can get myself to the hospital once this is dealt with."

I pulled the cell out my handbag, bringing up Detective Ortega's number. "Detective? This is Miss Mae Cooper. We were just attacked by a man with a knife. I think he's the person who's been sending the boxes, and Ziggy, my bodyguard, has him detained. Let me give you the address."

"Good work," said Ziggy once I finished the call. "Now I need you to call Sam, tell him we have a situation and need backup. Give him the address. Okay, Miss Cooper?"

"Got it." I repeated the process, giving Sam the details and address. Ziggy kept his gaze moving between the guy on the ground and our general surroundings the whole time. "Sam is on his way."

"Excellent. Good job."

"You're the one who did all the work."

"I wouldn't say that. Actually, I think we make a good team."

My smile was a weak tremulous thing.

"Now I want you to get in the vehicle, lock the doors, and remain in there until we've got more people on scene, okay?"

"No." I picked up my handbag and got back onto my feet. Though I retrieved a silk scarf out of it first. "Let me see the cut."

"Stay back please." Ziggy gave me his best I'm-very-serious-about-this eyes. "Do not come any closer."

"Give me your arm."

"Mae, it's not that bad and I need you safe. Don't worry about it."

"Blood is dripping off your fingers. Stop playing the tough guy and let me stop the bleeding before your arm falls off or something."

He just looked at me.

"I'm not going anywhere until you let me see it."

With a sigh, he held out the damaged limb. The knife had slashed through the suit and shirt, the cut a good hand's length at least. Whoa. Lots of blood. I wrapped the scarf around the wound, firmly but not too firm. At any rate, it seemed to be about the right amount of pressure to slow down the flow of red stuff. It'd been a number of years since I'd completed my first aid course at summer camp so I could only hope I'd done it right.

"It needs stitches. Doesn't seem to be too deep, but it's probably going to scar." I carefully tied off the knot. "However, that scarf's new season Chanel. It wouldn't surprise me if you're all better in an hour or two."

"Magical designer wear, huh?" He half smiled. So pretty. Made my heart beat hard for a whole new reason.

"What the hell is going on out here?" Lena ran toward me across the parking lot, followed fast by Zane.

"Oh my God." His eyes went wide at the sight of the man lying on the ground.

Guess the asshole took his failure to stab me pretty hard since he'd started crying. Or maybe it was due to his broken nose and busted balls. Hard to say.

Zane pulled a handkerchief out of his pocket and carefully picked up the bloody knife. "I'm guessing this will be needed for evidence. Goodness gracious. Wish I'd seen the bodyguard take him down. Bet that was exciting."

"He's the one who sent you those boxes?" asked Lena.

"Probably," I said. "It seems likely, doesn't it?"

Lena just blinked. "Oh, boy. Check out his cap…"

"Yeah, I saw. Guess he's a fanatic who thinks I broke the ex's heart or something. Hence all of the symbolism of sending me the lumps of dead bloody meat."

"Your ex sure does have some dedicated fans," said Zane. "I wonder if you can sue him over this for emotional distress or something. You probably can, you know? Or at least, sell your story and give a really dramatic interview. I could coach you, it'd be great. What do you think?"

I sighed. What a day. "Dude…no."

CHAPTER SEVEN

By the time Detective Ortega arrived with a couple of uniformed officers to take our statements and drag our attacker away, a couple of hours had gone by. Sam, Adelaide, and Bon arrived to help deal with the press then Bon took Ziggy to the hospital to get his arm looked at while Sam and Adelaide escorted me home. It all happened with military-like precision. These people knew their business.

Not that I didn't want to go to the hospital with Ziggy, but I wasn't really given the option. Sam firmly told me that my presence there would not be a good idea. Understandable. Calls and text messages were blowing up my phone all evening and well into the night. (Apart from letting Mom know I was okay, I ignored them.) If I'd gone with him to the hospital then there'd have been a media storm there which would not have been cool. The man needed his arm stitched up, not to have the spotlight thrust on him yet again.

So I'd gone home, taken off my make-up, and changed into some sweat pants and a battered "The Cure" T-shirt that hadn't seen better days since the previous century. It was my comfort clothing.

By this time, I felt reasonably mentally fortified enough to check out the situation on my cell. And what a clusterfuck it was. Video of the attack and Ziggy taking down the asshole had already gone viral. The thought of how close he'd come to being seriously injured kind of made me want to hurl.

"Interesting use of a head butt," said Sam, sitting on the couch opposite me with a cup of coffee in one hand and his cell in the other. God knows how many times he'd watched the footage.

Adelaide had remained downstairs in the lobby keeping an eye on the paparazzi out by the front door.

"Best get this to our lawyer in case the idiot tries for excessive force," he muttered, more to himself than me.

"Does that happen often?"

He gave me a small smile. "No, not often. And not when there's so much clear footage of the incident. He clearly came at you with a knife. There's no way a judge would fall for it."

"I don't want Ziggy getting into trouble because of me." I cradled my bottle of beer in two hands, huddled in the corner of the couch. "He's already been hurt."

"Miss Cooper, you didn't bring any of this on yourself. Ziggy did his job and did it well," said Sam. "Once the threat was dealt with, he waited calmly for the police to arrive and take charge of the scene. Nothing more."

I nodded.

"It'll be fine."

"Sure," I said, but I didn't really believe it.

No idea when I fell asleep exactly. I'd told Sam I'd be fine if he wanted to head home, but he'd stayed. Turned out he was into old black and white movies. Or maybe that was just his sneaky bodyguard trick to distract shocked clients with something safe and familiar. If so, it worked. Half way through Casablanca or so was about the last thing I remembered. Now there were voices, neither of which belonged to Bogart or Bergman.

"…injured, but also you're off the clock. Sure you should be here?" asked Sam.

"I'm fine," answered Ziggy.

"Not talking about your arm. I saw how you were looking at her last night and today."

Nothing from Ziggy.

"Figured you'd be coming by. That's why I waited around, to have a word with you."

"Regarding what?" asked Ziggy.

"You know it never works out, getting involved with a client. You've seen that before. We both have."

Oh, boy.

For a moment, no one said anything. Then Ziggy cleared his throat.

"You should go. Martha will be wondering where you are."

"She knows where I am. That's the thing about relationships…making them work is complicated. Takes a lot of effort," said Sam. "And if you're not committed to putting in serious effort, don't go there at all. Especially for someone you've known for what…a couple of days? Easy enough for a guy like you to find some company for the night without doing potential damage to my business and your reputation."

Ziggy sighed.

"She seems like a good woman."

"She is and I hear what you're saying, all right?"

"Right then," said Sam. "Good work today."

The front door clicked quietly closed.

Footsteps moved toward me, the couch shifting slightly with his weight as he sat. "You should be in bed." His voice was quiet, contemplative. "You're not going to get a decent sleep on the couch."

I slowly opened my eyes and stretched. "Hey. How'd you do at the hospital?"

"Fine. Why aren't you in bed instead of crashing out here?"

"You're not the boss of me." I sat up, pushing my hair out of my face. Odds were I looked like roadkill, but whatever. "Show me your arm."

He angled his body slightly, displaying the white bandage peeking out from beneath the edge of his black tee and going down almost to his elbow. The suit and so on were gone. Guess his clothes had been stained with blood. Now he wore jeans and sneakers. A much more relaxed look though every bit as hot as the suits. "Eighteen stitches. Not much to see."

"That's a lot of stitches."

"And I didn't even cry once."

"You're such a tough guy."

"That's why you pay me." He rose to his feet, keeping his gaze averted. "Okay, Miss Cooper. You've seen my owie. Time for you to get to bed and for me to go home."

"Where is home, you never said?"

And apparently he wasn't going to say now, either. Right. Privacy and all that. Professionalism. It was important. I didn't need personal details about this man no matter how much I might like to have them.

Today, the lines had gotten a little blurred. But it was time to put them firmly back in place. Boundaries mattered.

I got to my feet, noting how much smaller I seemed standing next to his bulk. Weird. Yet my heart felt about a billion times bigger and heavier than normal. Maybe I was coming down with the flu. It was as good an excuse as any. A love sickness of some sort seemed the most likely. Stupid me. "Ziggy, I just wanted to say that I'm sorry you got hurt today because of me. And thank you for stopping him. I'd probably be deceased right now if you hadn't been there."

A nod.

This was good. This was for the best. Him being distant and professional. Me not being a hot mess. On the outside at least. It would be best for everyone concerned if this thing between us never got started. That would be the adult, smart thing to do.

"Sam said Adelaide would be available to take over for the next few days," I said. "So you can have some time off."

"I told him that wouldn't be necessary."

"I, um, I think it is a good idea." So many feelings. It hurt to hold them all inside.

"Respectfully, Miss Cooper, I do not need time off." He sounded stern times a thousand. Ziggy Thayer was an unhappy boy indeed. "I am more than capable of continuing to do my job."

"I've made up my mind," I said, turning my back on him. Dammit. My bottom lip had turned traitor and started to tremble. My eyes were welling with tears. Not helpful at all. I blinked furiously, forcing it all back down.

"May I ask why?"

"Why?"

"Yes. Why?"

"Why the hell do you think?" What an idiotic specimen of the male species. Seriously. I spun back around with a frown in place. "Because you got hurt today. Because of me."

His gaze narrowed. "Are you crying?"

"No." I wiped away a tear with the back of my hand. "Don't be ridiculous. You can go now."

"I'm not leaving you when you're upset."

"Well, I'm not going to stop being upset until you leave."

He raised a brow. "Guess we've got a problem then."

"You're serious? Seriously? You're refusing to leave?"

"That's right."

"Enough. I'm done." Give me strength. I pointed my finger at him in a very hostile manner. "You, Ziggy Thayer, are frustrating and annoying and confusing and I don't like you very much right now so you should leave and not come back for several days."

"That so?"

"Yes, I...stop questioning everything."

"How else am I going to find things out?"

I looked to heaven. Then I crossed my arms over my chest because even the flimsiest of defenses was better than nothing. "What things exactly do you need to find out? Actually, don't answer that. I don't want to know. Good night."

He cocked his head, leveling me with that stare.

"What?"

"You're allowed to ask questions and I'm not?"

"Oh my God," I groaned. "How much blood exactly did you lose because honestly you're kind of acting crazy?"

"Yeah, I know. You should probably make a complaint about me. Want me to fetch your cell so you can call Sam?"

"You think I won't?"

"I honestly have no idea what you're going to do, Mae." He took a deep breath. "I had every intention of coming in here, checking you were fine, then leaving. That's it."

I shrugged. "So what happened?"

"Then you started talking. Then you got upset. And now...I don't know." There was no professional blank to his face now. If anything, the man seemed to be holding back an excess of emotion. His lips were a fine line, his brow furrowed. "This is the problem, whenever I'm around you, every rational thought goes straight out the damn window. I honestly don't know if I'm coming or going."

I gasped in outrage. "Me? What did I do?"

"Just walking around breathing and being you, mostly."

"That makes absolutely no sense."

"I know," he said, voice resigned. "Funny you should say that thing about how frustrating and annoying and confusing I am. Because that's exactly how I feel about you."

"But I'm just a job to you. You shouldn't have feelings for me."

"Wish to hell I didn't. It'd make things a fuck of a lot less complicated."

I just stared.

"I like my life how it is," he continued. "I've got work and family and friends. It's all good. Maybe in five or ten years I'd be interested in marriage and kids, but not now. Let alone not with someone like you."

"Someone like me?"

"That's right."

A fiery rage burned within. "Good news, Ziggy. I don't recall either proposing to you or offering to bear your spawn. You're free to go, buddy. The door's right there. Don't let it hit your ass on the way out!"

The man just smiled. Like I wasn't about to attack him with my perfect French nail polish. Scour his face with lines and all the rest. What's worse was, as soon as I saw his smile, my knees turned to water. Oh, man.

"Mae, I spend enough time dealing with photographers and fans at work. Of course I was wary of inviting that sort of thing into my private life," he said. "However, it's a part of your life and that's good enough for me. But you should know, I'm never going to be able to buy you a Bentley or take you on a private jet to Paris. Often I have to work late or travel. No matter how much I want to, I'm not always going to be able to be with you. Can you accept that?"

"You've given this a lot of thought."

"It's pretty much the only thing I've been thinking about since I met you."

And that was big. That was really big. Scarily huge, in fact.

"So what do you say?" he asked calmly. "We could try just fucking, see if we lose interest in each other. But I honestly don't think that's going to happen anytime soon."

"Huh."

He waited. I stared. Not much else happened. "Mae, it's been a shit of a day. And as much fun as this is, I'm exhausted and so are you. What do you say we call it a night and if you want, we can keep arguing some more about it in the morning over breakfast?"

I had nothing.

"I'll sleep in the chair in your room again. No need to rush things. You can think everything over and let me know when you reach a decision. No pressure, okay?"

My head was a mess.

"Fact of it is, I can't walk away from you. Already tried going home instead of coming here tonight."

"You did?"

"Yeah, knew it was the smart thing to do. But I couldn't do it."

"I would have been so worried." It was nothing less than the truth. "Probably wouldn't have slept at all. I mean, I would have understood, but…"

He nodded. "I know. I needed to see you too."

I stood there, thinking deep thoughts. My head was a mess and my heart wasn't much better. Though at the heart of the matter, the man had a point. In fact, he had several of them.

"What do you say, Miss Cooper?"

I raised my chin. "You know I hate it when you call me that?"

"Yes, I do."

My gaze narrowed and he smiled again. Such an ass. A smokin' hot one, though. Along with being smart, funny, sweet, and brave. Oh God, I was on the verge of swooning. Game over. "So let me get this straight. My options are, have sex with you, or have sex and attempt a relationship with you?"

"Or there's number three," he said. "We go back to being purely professional and never talk about this again. If you'd feel more comfortable, I can have Sam bring in someone else to watch you until the paparazzi leave you alone and you don't require our services anymore. Whatever you choose, I would still like to crash here tonight. You'd feel safer and get a decent night's sleep and I'd feel better knowing you weren't alone and freaking out after everything that's happened. I can even sleep out here on the couch if you'd prefer instead of in your room."

"But you're off the clock, Sam said so."

"I'm not here to get paid, Mae. I'm here because of you."

CHAPTER EIGHT

He was here because of me. What did you do with a man who always put you first? It was honestly kind of a new experience.

Slowly, I stepped forward. One step, two, three, until we were almost touching. He smelled good. Cologne and heat and him. I could have gotten high off the smell. "Can I kiss you?"

"Sweetness, you can do whatever you want with me."

Good enough for me. I raised up on tippy toes and he leaned down and we met in the middle. My hands fisted in his shirt as his mouth met mine. Warm, firm lips. Very nice. At first, I was hesitant. Or I guess we both were. The kiss was soft, exploratory. His breath against my mouth and his lips pressing against mine over and over. It was a sweet, chaste, and pure kind of thing and I could have done it with him for days. Though, to be honest, there were also better things we could have been doing. So I was the dirty girl who had to bring tongue into it. His lips automatically opened and oh yes. I moaned and his hands clasped my waist, holding me close. Like I'd been trying to escape. Get real.

Our tongues entwined and his fingers dug into my back, then my butt. Also, something was definitely making its presence felt against my hip. And it was a sizeable appendage by the feel of things. Or at least one very intent on getting my attention.

"Sorry," he muttered, eyes hazy with lust. "Adrenaline from the fight."

I drew back from him another inch or two, catching my breath, trying to still my dizzy head. That kind of thing. Except when I looked down between us at the lump in his pants, my excitement levels skyrocketed all over again. If I didn't get to see it, I would not go to bed happy. So that decided that.

"We don't have to go any further than you're comfortable with," he said, licking his lips. "I'm still okay with sleeping on that chair. Or I can leave if you want some space."

"I don't think I need space right now and I definitely don't want you sleeping in the chair. You got hurt today."

His smile was all sorts of soft and gentle. "I'm fine. You don't need to worry about that. You just kissed me all better."

"Hmm. That's sweet. But you're missing the point. The thing is, if we're going to be sharing a bed, I'm pretty certain things are going to happen."

"After that kiss, you're probably right."

"So do you have a condom?"

He swallowed. "Yes."

"Next question. Are you the kind of guy who judges girls for wanting to have sex on the first date? Not that we've even actually been on a date yet. But you get my meaning."

"Fuck no. I try not to be a hypocritical douchebag whenever possible."

"Good answer. Follow me."

I turned and headed down the hallway. First off came my old tee. Next went my oh so glamorous sweatpants. Handy thing about having your own lingerie line, you tend to have a lot of nice underwear. Tonight's set was black hipster panties and a matching bra with delicate embroidery and lace cups. By the muttered profanity behind me, he liked them a lot. There was much to be said for boldness. Screw my foibles and insecurities. Ziggy wanted me and I wanted him and then some. Time to enjoy the moment and worry about the rest later.

I looked back over my shoulder at the bedroom door. My man was busy hopping along, pulling off a sneaker and sock. The other sneaker and sock were already littering the hallway. Sometimes it was fun to make a mess. Then he tore his T-shirt off over his head, exposing his gorgeous body to me. All of that skin I wanted to touch and taste. My fingers itched, my mouth started to water. If it weren't for the bandage, so white against his tanned skin, everything would have been perfect.

"Don't worry about it." He cupped my face, gently kissing my lips. "I'm fine and I'm feeling better by the moment. Must have been that

Chanel scarf of yours."

I smiled. "Are you mocking my designer accessories?"

"Never."

My hand slipped behind his neck, bringing his mouth back to mine. We kissed deep and hard and wet for a good long time. Who even needed oxygen or coherent thoughts? So overrated. His lips travelled over my jaw and down my neck, seeking out all of my sensitive spots. Some tickled. Some turned me on. All of it was good. Only when he gripped my waist and went to lift me did I crash back to Earth.

"Ziggy, no," I said in a rush. "You'll bust your stitches."

He growled and rested his forehead against mine. "Sweetness, not to be crass or anything, but I'd dearly love to fuck you against this door."

"That's a nice idea. But neither of us wants to spend the night back in emergency."

"True," he grumped. "But I would like your legs wrapped around me. Mind if we head for the bed?"

"Actually, I've got a better and slightly safer idea that still involves the nice soft bed." I tore open the top button of his jeans, lowered the zipper. Nice and careful-like I inched his jeans down over his hips and ass. "What if you lie down on your back and I climb on top of you? That way you won't be holding yourself up or anything and there won't be any pressure on your wound."

"Okay." He sighed. "I'm sorry this isn't more spontaneous and wild."

"Eh. We can do crazy monkey sex another time when you're not hurt."

"Promise?" he asked, planting a kiss on my lips.

"Promise. Now get on the bed already."

His answering chuckle made my pussy clench. I swear. Even careful sex with this man might kill me. But it would be an awesome way to go.

"Just a minute," he said, reaching around me to undo my bra. The straps slid down my shoulders and his eyes were huge, taking in my breasts. "I've been dreaming about these."

"Have you?"

"Every fucking night. Your ass, your tits, your hair, your smile. Hell, your baking and hanging out in sweats. Everything about you gets to me." His thumbs brushed over my nipples, turning hard to *oh my*

God. He took their weight in each hand, massaging and squeezing. The man had large and capable hands. I thought I was in love. When he bent low to suck on my nipples, taking turns flicking and teasing them with his tongue, I shuddered and almost came. My panties were damp, clinging to the lips of my sex. Crazy town.

"You need to get on the bed," I said, voice somewhat shaky. "Now."

"Whatever you say." Ziggy hustled off his jeans, his thumbs in the waistband of his navy boxer briefs. The outline of his cock without the denim in the way was even more impressive. "These too, Miss Cooper?"

"Hurry it up."

At this, he outright grinned. Making this man smile was my new life goal. Except, instead of dragging down his underwear, he stopped and searched a pocket of his discarded jeans. Out came his wallet and inside were a string of three condoms. "I get checked regularly. Never have sex without protection. But we'll go out tomorrow for more, okay?"

"First thing," I agreed. "And I got checked for everything under the sun, moon, and stars after my ex. I'm clean."

He nodded and tossed the prophylactics on the bed before dragging down his boxer briefs. A perfect cock sprang forth, swollen thick and lined with veins. Thank you, Baby Jesus. This man was mine. I reached out to touch, but he took a step back, climbing onto the bed with that grin again. Flat on his back, he took himself in hand and pumped once, twice. "You've still got your panties on, Mae. You're getting left behind."

"Don't you dare start without me, Ziggy Thayer."

"I can't help if you're being so damn slow."

Mid-panty divesting, I kind of almost unfortunately lost my balance. Hopping on one foot, almost falling on my ass in front of my new boyfriend/lover/whatever he was wasn't my finest moment. "Oh, man. I'm such a klutz."

"Are you kidding me?" he asked, still playing with himself, which wasn't fair at all. "Watching your breasts bounce like that was every Christmas and birthday come at once. Do it again."

I bit back a smile. He'd always seemed so serious. Yet sex with Ziggy was fun and we hadn't even gotten to the actual sex part yet. Certainly I felt way more comfortable with him than I had with anyone in a long time. This was shaping up to be a spectacular end to a truly crappy day. An end I hoped to repeat with him often.

Without preamble, I grabbed the string of condoms and tore one free, ripping into the wrapping with my teeth. His gaze darkened, his hand moving away from his dick. I threw a leg over, sitting on his hairy thighs. Nice and muscular legs, by the way. As I wrapped my fingers around his cock, white pre-cum dribbled from the top. Good that he'd confirmed he was clean. I swiped it up with a thumb and stuck it in my mouth. Yummy and salty. This man made me hungry in all the ways.

"Fuck," he muttered. "Put it on me, sweetness. I think I've waited long enough."

"It's only been a few minutes."

"No. It's been days."

I smiled and rolled the condom down over his rigid shaft. Then, leaning forward on my hands, I kissed him on the lips. The man wasted no time in tangling his hands in my hair and soul kissing me. My breasts brushed against his hard chest, my wet pussy teasing the head of his cock. Rubbing against him lit me up inside in the most beautiful way. Finally, I could take no more, holding him steady and lining him up with my entrance.

"Eyes on me," he said.

I did as asked, pushing down, taking him deep inside. And he fit just right. About average length, but nice and thick. Hands gripped my hips, holding me steady.

"Be careful with that arm," I reminded him, sounding slightly breathy. Exactly how a sex goddess should sound, really. The way he looked at me, the heat in his eyes, let me know he loved what he saw and then some.

Slowly I rose up before sinking back down, building a gradual rhythm. Enough to tease us both, stoking the fires without rushing. His hands rose to my breasts, squeezing and massaging them once more. It all felt so good. Heat built, sliding straight through my veins. It wasn't easy keeping my eyes open. When I leaned forward a little and his cock hit something awesome inside of me, my mouth dropped open on a gasp. Ziggy's hands returned to my hips, guiding me back to that same place over and over. I placed my palms flat against his pecs, not losing my balance again but holding myself steady. Doing my best to hold myself together when everything seemed to be getting ready to fly apart.

"That's it," he said, voice rough and low.

All I could do was nod.

Sweat slicked both our skins and my blood hummed. It was so good, riding him, watching him, feeling him move beneath me. The determined expression on his face, the absolute focus on me. It was intense and perfect and my adrenaline surged. My knees dug into his sides, my body moving fast and sure. And his hands on me urged me on. Faster, harder, and more.

So much more.

Then he licked his fingertips and reached down between my legs, searching out my clit. Around and over he worked the tight bud, urging me higher and higher. When I came, I came hard. Stars burst behind my eyelids, pure sensation burst through me, breaking me apart. Fingers digging into my ass, he slammed himself up into me once, twice, three times more before slowly stilling.

Lucky for me, he didn't seem to mind having me sprawled across his chest. His heart hammered beneath my ear and perspiration glued us together. The room seemed humid, smelling of sex. Eau de Ziggy and me. Fingers slid up and down my spine, but his eyelids remained closed. Everything was peaceful. After the rough last couple of days, it was exactly what I needed.

Traces of dark stubble lined his jaw, almost hiding a faint white scar. There was another on his shoulder. A couple on his chest.

"What are you thinking about?" he asked softly.

"Nothing much. I'm just happy that you're here."

He opened his eyelids, resting an arm behind his head like a pillow. "I never stood a chance with you, did I?"

"How so?"

"Not only are you drop dead fucking gorgeous, you're too damn sweet for words."

"Oh, really? So you think I'm hot when I'm mooching around in sweats with no makeup and crappy hair?"

"You mean when you're all relaxed and chilling at home, baking shit and reading books?" he asked. "I'm delighted to tell you you're insanely hot then. But of course you're also hot when you're on a shoot and made up to the nines with your hair all fancy. And when you've just come so hard you almost broke my dick, you are scorching hot."

I did not blush. The room was just warm.

"Face it, you're hot all the time. It's the truth."

"Hmm. I think you're biased."

"I think I'm the lucky bastard that gets to worship the ground a benevolent goddess walks on." The look in his eyes was most meaningful. Amused, almost.

"I knew it." I rose up, letting him slide out of me. When I tried to climb off the bed, however, he grabbed my wrist in a loose but unbreakable hold. "I knew you were listening when Lena and I were talking. Ziggy, that was a private conversation."

"Then don't have it eight feet away from me talking at the top of your voices next time." He smirked, pressing a kiss to the inside of my wrist before letting go. "I'm not going to apologize for listening. That was useful information. Mind if I use the bathroom?"

"No, go ahead."

He kissed my bare shoulder and away he went. "There's like five hundred tubes and jars of stuff in here. Enough for a dozen women."

"Get used to it."

"Yes, Miss Cooper."

Such a smartass of a man. The bathroom door softly clicked shut. Truth be known, I don't think I'd stood much of a chance against him either. Handsome, capable, had his shit together. Behaved like an actual grown-up most of the time and had no sexual shenanigans currently showing on YouTube. Yes, I'd searched. Once bitten, twice shy and all that. He even thought I was hot in all of my various moods and modes. To all intents and purposes, I'd hit the maybe boyfriend jackpot. Actually, I should probably get some specifics on that.

"Ziggy?" I wandered closer to the door.

Inside the bathroom, the toilet flushed. "Yeah?"

"Sorry to disturb you, but...quick question," I said. "Are we dating now? I mean, are we like together? You know, boyfriend/girlfriend or partner or whatever type of—"

"Mae."

"No pressure. I'm just curious."

"We're together, okay? We're working this out."

"Okay."

"I'm going to wash my hands. Be out in a minute."

"Sure. Go ahead."

A tap turned on.

We were official. Glad we had that sorted. Now I just had to stop or at least learn to ignore the weird feeling going on in my stomach. Hopefully it would go away. It was a sickly churning heavy kind of sensation. An uncomfortable weight in my middle, like a premonition everything was somehow about to go wrong. Which was stupid because it wasn't. We'd just had spectacular sex. He was laughing and happy and stating in specific terms that we were together. My stalker was behind bars for the foreseeable future. All was good and right in my world.

I studied my somewhat glowing post-great-sex face in the mirror beside the bed. "Knock it off," I whisper-hissed. "Everything is fine."

But even though Ziggy held me in his arms all night long and I actually slept, the feeling didn't go away. Dammit.

Dicks were kind of fascinating. I wrapped my hand around Ziggy's the next morning, feeling the heat, breathing in the musky scent. Waking up to bacon and eggs was great. Waking up to Ziggy naked before having bacon and eggs was even better.

"Sweetness," he sleepily muttered. "What are you up to?"

In lieu of a response, I sucked on his cockhead. No messing around. My tongue massaged the tip of his penis, digging in a little to the hole before circling the ridge. At this, he muttered a few other interesting things, his hands tangling in my hair. Taking him deeper, I rubbed my tongue up and down his swelling shaft. Below where I was working, my fingers grasped and stroked the rest of his length.

We'd used up the remaining two condoms during the night. Whenever I woke up from a bad dream, he was there, ready to put my world to rights. Nothing like an orgasm to put a smile back on a girl's face. Since I still wouldn't let him be on top and risk busting any stitches, we'd done it doggy style and lying spooning on our sides. I had a feeling sex wouldn't be a problem in our relationship anytime in the near future. Honestly, after the night before, I was a little sore in the very best way.

But back to sucking cock.

I firmed my lips and worked them up and down, taking turns to flick across his cockhead with my tongue. With my hand below keeping up the rhythm, he started pulsing in no time. Seemed his whole body tensed and the way he said my name, like it was something holy. It was very nice to hear. Finally his dick jerked, cum flooding the back of my throat. I swallowed it down fast, easing up on my attentions as he slowly came down.

"Okay?" I asked, stroking his thighs and flat stomach.

In response, he grabbed me beneath the arms and dragged me up onto his chest. Then he held me tight, his heavy breaths ruffling the hair on top of my head. Fingers dug into the sides of my spine, massaging up and down its length. Finally, he lifted my hair and rubbed the back of my neck. Magic fingers worked my muscles into mush. The man had many talents.

"Good morning, sweetness," he said, voice husky.

I kissed his pec. "Morning."

Which was when someone started hammering on the damn front door.

"Why does God hate me?" I mock cried.

"I'll get it." He carefully rolled me onto the mattress then jumped off, pulling on jeans before going in search of his T-shirt. Probably it lay somewhere in the hall where he'd abandoned it last night.

I followed my bodyguard boyfriend somewhat more slowly, pulling on a blue silk robe. Probably time I got busy with the bacon and eggs. Lord knows, my stomach was growling. We'd worked off some serious calories through the night. Ziggy gave me an even better workout than Kwana. God bless him.

Familiar female voices came from the living room.

"I'll just put it over on the counter," said Lena. "No need to wake her up."

"Yes, Mrs. Ferris."

"The croissants can just be warmed up a little in the oven if she likes." That was Ev. "Oh, we should pop the juice in the fridge."

"Good idea," said Lena.

"Hey." I raised my hand in greeting. "What's all this?"

Lena rushed toward me, giving me a fierce hug. "I'm so glad you're okay. Thank goodness Ziggy was there to stop that lunatic from hurting you."

"I'm fine." I patted her on the back. "Really. He's the one that got hurt. Hi, Ev. Thank you so much for all this, you guys. Is this all from your café?"

Ev smiled, a takeout coffee in hand. "It is. And it's the least we can do after everything you've been through. I'm so glad you're okay."

Ziggy stood near the closed door, T-shirt, jeans, and sneakers in place. Along with his professional face. He stood straight and tall, hand hanging loose by his side. No one would suspect a thing. Surely. Not that I was embarrassed by my new relationship with Ziggy. But I wasn't sure when and how he wanted it to become public knowledge. But also, when something was this new, you kind of wanted to just enjoy it privately for a while.

The phone rang, the little button for reception lighting up. Ziggy answered it in a low voice before putting a hand over the receiver.

"What is it?" I asked.

Something in his jaw jumped. "Your ex is downstairs."

"My ex?"

His nod was a sharp jerk.

"Huh." I pondered the situation for all of half a second. It was tempting to send him on his way without giving him a minute of my time. That's probably what he deserved, but still... "Ask them to send him up please."

He paused, quickly burying whatever he felt about the situation. "Whatever you want, Miss Cooper."

Oh yeah. This morning was going just great. But fuck it, it was time to face my demons.

Lena stepped back with a worried frown on her face. "Do you want us to go, or..."

"No. It's fine," I decided. "This shouldn't take long."

"Whatever you say." Lena grabbed a coffee too and made herself at home on the couch. Ev soon sat down beside her.

Ziggy hadn't relaxed any. Guess I could understand that. Maybe he was a smidgeon jealous. I certainly didn't look forward to ever meeting any of his exes (but you could bet I'd do it wearing Louboutins). Or maybe he'd already stopped one crazy person with a knife from getting at me this week. The ex had done a lot of damage to me without being allowed a second swing now. Though maybe this time things could be different. Thing is, I'd never know unless I tried. And I really wanted to try.

When the knock came, Ziggy opened the door without a word.

In the ex stepped, every bit the big-ass quarterback I remembered. He pretty much dominated any and every room he entered. The dude always seem to loom. Not that I'd ever been scared of him or anything.

He and his ego just took up a lot of space. There was, however, an impressive display of concern going on with the tight lips and soft eyes. He looked around at those assembled before once again fixing on me. "Mae. Babe."

"Uh!" I held up a finger. "That's enough. Let me guess, what with the flowers you sent and then the news about your little fan boy attacking me yesterday, you thought you'd ride on over here and save the day. Is that right?"

He blinked. "Mae. Babe."

"You already said that. Try something new."

"I just wanted to make sure you were okay. Scared the crap out of me, hearing you'd been attacked."

"Uh-huh." I grabbed one of the almond croissants out of the goodie bag and ripped off a piece. "What else have you got?"

"What else have I got? What do you mean?" He gave me his gosh ma'am smile. "I missed you. I'm worried about you. Isn't that good enough?"

I scrunched up my nose. "No. Not really."

Now he did his awkward nervous chuckle, gaze slipping over the assembled audience. It stopped on Ziggy. Then the ex's eyes narrowed into a mean slit. "Who's this guy?"

"My new boyfriend."

"I knew that was sex hair." Lena just about jumped out of her chair. "You look like a well-pleasured mess this morning and I've never been more proud of you."

I laughed. "Thank you."

Ziggy quietly groaned.

Ev just smiled and took another sip of coffee. She really had the Mona Lisa smile thing down.

"You're fucking your bodyguard?" asked the ex, disgust dripping from every word. Such a schmuck.

"You're going to judge? You? Really?" I set my hands on my hips. "Anyway, doesn't matter. I only let you up here to say what I need to say, then you're gone. Done with. Kaput."

Now he looked cranky. It wasn't like people said no to him often, the big football baby. Ziggy took a step closer. But I was fine. Hell, I was on fire.

"I forgive you," I said. "Most important though, I forgive myself.

For letting your bullshit opinions mess with my self-confidence. For putting your lies inside my head. For allowing you to make me feel even an inch like less than the queen that I am. For giving you a second of my precious time during this one wild and precious life."

"Oh, well said." Ev set down her coffee and started clapping. "Bravo."

"Seconded," added Lena.

"Excellent use of Mary Oliver, too."

"Yeah, I noticed that. Nice touch."

"Thank you, ladies." I smiled. "I was rather proud with how it shaped up myself."

Ziggy hid a smirk behind his hand.

"What the fuck, Mae?" The ex's fingers clenched into fists. His happiness levels had definitely taken a plunge. "Have you lost your damn mind?"

"No, I lost you. And it was the best damn thing that ever happened to me." I pointed at the door. "Now get out. You're neither wanted nor welcome."

"I was good to you."

"You were shit. But it doesn't matter anymore."

"What?" he sneered. "Because you're fucking the hired help?"

"No. Because I'm over you. I have been for a while." I sighed. "If I hadn't met Ziggy, I still wouldn't want a damn thing to do with you. You're nothing more than human rubbish. Now kindly take yourself out to the curb."

The ex sputtered, his face turning a particularly vibrant shade of red. It was a wondrous sight. Truly. Something I'd treasure until my dying day.

Ziggy stepped forward. "The lady asked you to leave."

And while the ex might have been big and built, I wouldn't give him a chance against someone like Ziggy. Happily and somewhat surprisingly, he seemed intelligent enough to understand that much at least. The sound of the door slamming after him will reverberate in the happy depths of my soul unto my dying day.

I breathed out. "Wow."

"Feel better?" he asked, coming up nice and close to me.

"Much. It's amazing really. I feel lighter, almost. Like I'd been carrying something around and I didn't even realize it."

He just smiled. "I'm glad."

"You two are so cute together." Lena happy sighed. "Honestly, just, you look great together. Would you mind if I took some pictures? Just for your private collection, of course."

"We should leave," said Ev, dragging the other woman out of her chair. "We should go so Mae and Ziggy can have some privacy and breakfast and whatever."

"Oh, okay. Mae, call me later."

"I will call you later," I dutifully replied.

The door finally closed behind the two women, and Ziggy and I were alone. At last. Just me and my new man, who looked particularly fetching with his stubble and all.

"Thank you," I said. "You helped get me back to myself. Everything that's happened…I guess I just really see what I let that idiot do to my head now."

"All those doubts gone?"

"Yeah. I think they really are." I slid my arms around him, resting my head against his chest. "You want to be happy with me, Ziggy Thayer?"

"Let me tell you something," he said, kissing the top of my head. "Miss Cooper, I already am."

EPILOGUE

The door clicked open, Ziggy stepping into the apartment. "Why wasn't that door locked?"

"Because Leonard let me know you were on your way up." I sucked some chocolate frosting off a finger and gave him my wickedest smile. "Also, that's a shitty way to greet your woman after you've been gone for five long days, Mister Thayer."

"I'll take seeing to your safety over niceties any day of the week, sweetness." He turned the alarm system back on and locked the door. "You know that."

"Hmm."

He moved toward me like the big predator he was. "I missed you."

"Did you now?"

"I did. Did you miss me?"

I smiled again. "You absence might not have gone entirely unnoticed."

"Kind of you. That why you're making my favorite cake?" He stepped around the kitchen island, sliding an arm around my waist. The man still wore a black suit like nobody's business. Playing it cool after he'd been gone for a week was a tough ask, in all honesty. He kissed my cheek, lips lingering against my skin. One big hand slid over my left butt cheek. "Or is that why you're wearing nothing but a skimpy chemise beneath that apron?"

"Maybe. How was life on tour?" I asked, craning my neck to give him better access.

"Honestly, I've had enough Country and Western music to last me a lifetime."

Ziggy had moved in with me all of about five seconds after we got together. Not that it was official or anything for the first few months. But if he wasn't at work, he was here with me. So keeping his apartment across town seemed pretty silly pretty fast. He only took away jobs for a week maximum before swapping out with another bodyguard so he could come home. His choice, not mine. Though it was nice to know he made us a priority. It wasn't always easy, what with the long hours. However, we made it work. For me, the man was more than worth it and I guess he felt the same. Sometimes I had to go to L.A. or New York for work and if he was available, he went with me. If not, we talked and texted whenever possible. While his boss, Sam, reportedly hadn't been delighted at our coupledom, he'd come around to the idea of Ziggy and me being serious. There were certainly no weird scenes or vibes at any of the Stage Dive etcetera get-togethers. Life was good. Very good.

"Hello there. Is that a gun in your pocket or are you just happy to see me?" I asked when he ground something suspiciously hard against my hip. Hard and vaguely box like in shape so sadly not his magnificent dick.

The man instantly stilled. "You weren't supposed to notice that."

"Oh?"

"Let's pretend you didn't notice it." Something in his gaze seemed almost…damn, I wasn't sure what the emotion was. Which made me even more curious.

"I don't think so. Hand it over."

"Sweetness…"

"Gimme." I slipped my hand into his pants pocket, drawing out the small blue box. As always when he was coming home from a job, he wore a gun in a holster beneath his arm. But I'd gotten used to that. This Tiffany box, however, was something quite new. "You bought me jewelry? It's not my birthday for months yet."

"I know. This isn't for your birthday."

I popped the lid on the box, eyes going wide as twin moons at the sight of the diamond solitaire ring sitting within. "Holy shit."

"Agreed," he muttered. "Meant to hide it in the car. But I was rushing to get back to you and forgot. I had plans for how this was going to go down."

"Ziggy, that's a really big ring. Like seriously huge."

"Had Lena use the Ferris name to get us a table at the fancy new restaurant in town you've been wanting to try, but has been booked out for months."

"It's so shiny." I took it out of the box, sliding it onto my ring finger. "See how shiny and pretty it is?"

"There was going to be roses and music. It was all going to be very romantic. You're getting chocolate frosting on the ring." He laughed quietly against my ear. "But I'm glad you like it."

"Hold up," I said, turning on him. "Did you actually just give me an engagement ring without telling me you love me first? Because I'll have you know, that's not the correct order these things are done in. My mother would be appalled at your lack of decorum."

"To be fair, you stole the ring straight out of my pocket. Like I keep saying, I had plans…" He winced. "But also, you mother loves me. I'll have *you* know, I already asked for her blessing and she happily gave it."

"You called my mom and asked for her permission?"

"I did."

"That's so nice." I grinned. "You're a nice man, Ziggy Thayer."

He tried giving me his hard-ass blank face expression, but it didn't work. "To be honest, I was a little worried you'd think it was too soon. But I don't know, it just felt right to me. You feel right to me, my mighty benevolent goddess."

"It's not too soon," I said, eyes getting misty. "Though you still haven't said that you love me. Like, ever."

The twin slashes of his dark brows drew together. "Haven't I?"

"No. Not once." I lightly poked him in the shoulder. "I've told you, Ziggy, but you have yet to say it back."

"I could have sworn I had."

"Nope. To be honest, it's been bugging me more than a little. But I decided to give it another week before I kicked your ass over it."

"You've been cranky about that and you still made my favorite chocolate cake for me anyway?"

"What can I say? I'm a sucker for you."

"The feeling's entirely mutual."

The ties on my apron loosened, the chocolate-smudged material falling to the ground at our feet. His hands cupped my face, mine sitting on his broad shoulders. "Here's the thing…I love you, Mae, and I have no fucking clue what I did without you all those years. You're my home, my whole damn world. You give me peace and happiness and I promise to always love and respect you and treat you like the queen that you are. I'm telling you now, you can trust me. Always."

"You're going to make me cry."

"Don't cry, sweetness," he murmured. "I'm not finished yet. Now I know you're already wearing the ring, but I'll ask anyway so there's no confusion. Will you marry me?"

"Yes, Ziggy. As a matter of fact, I will."

"Thank you."

"You're very welcome." I sniffed. "That was quite poetic, you know? Very romantic."

"Glad you approve. Enough talking now." Then he smiled and kissed me. A soul deep, world falling away, perfection in and of itself kind of kiss that could never be forgotten. My toes curled and my heart happy-sighed. And we did no more talking for a good long while.

* * * *

Also from Kylie Scott and 1001 Dark Nights, discover Strong.

Sign up for the 1001 Dark Nights Newsletter
and be entered to win a Tiffany Key necklace.

There's a contest every month!

Go to www.1001DarkNights.com to subscribe.

**As a bonus, all subscribers can download
FIVE FREE exclusive books!**

Discover 1001 Dark Nights Collection Six

DRAGON CLAIMED by Donna Grant
A Dark Kings Novella

ASHES TO INK by Carrie Ann Ryan
A Montgomery Ink: Colorado Springs Novella

ENSNARED by Elisabeth Naughton
An Eternal Guardians Novella

EVERMORE by Corinne Michaels
A Salvation Series Novella

VENGEANCE by Rebecca Zanetti
A Dark Protectors/Rebels Novella

ELI'S TRIUMPH by Joanna Wylde
A Reapers MC Novella

CIPHER by Larissa Ione
A Demonica Underworld Novella

RESCUING MACIE by Susan Stoker
A Delta Force Heroes Novella

ENCHANTED by Lexi Blake
A Masters and Mercenaries Novella

TAKE THE BRIDE by Carly Phillips
A Knight Brothers Novella

INDULGE ME by J. Kenner
A Stark Ever After Novella

THE KING by Jennifer L. Armentrout
A Wicked Novella

QUIET MAN by Kristen Ashley
A Dream Man Novella

ABANDON by Rachel Van Dyken
A Seaside Pictures Novella

THE OPEN DOOR by Laurelin Paige
A Found Duet Novella

CLOSER by Kylie Scott
A Stage Dive Novella

SOMETHING JUST LIKE THIS by Jennifer Probst
A Stay Novella

BLOOD NIGHT by Heather Graham
A Krewe of Hunters Novella

TWIST OF FATE by Jill Shalvis
A Heartbreaker Bay Novella

MORE THAN PLEASURE YOU by Shayla Black
A More Than Words Novella

WONDER WITH ME by Kristen Proby
A With Me In Seattle Novella

THE DARKEST ASSASSIN by Gena Showalter
A Lords of the Underworld Novella

Also from 1001 Dark Nights:
DAMIEN by J. Kenner

ABOUT KYLIE SCOTT

Kylie is a New York Times and USA Today best-selling author. She was voted Australian Romance Writer of the year, 2013, 2014, & 2018 by the Australian Romance Writers' Association and her books have been translated into eleven different languages.

DISCOVER MORE KYLIE SCOTT

Strong: A Stage Dive Novella
By Kylie Scott

When the girl of your dreams is kind of a nightmare.

As head of security to Stage Dive, one of the biggest rock bands in the world, Sam Knowles has plenty of experience dealing with trouble. But spoilt brat Martha Nicholson just might be the worst thing he's ever encountered. The beautiful troublemaker claims to have reformed, but Sam knows better than to think with what's in his pants. Unfortunately, it's not so easy to make his heart fall into line.

Martha's had her sights on the seriously built bodyguard for years. Quiet and conservative, he's not even remotely her type. So why the hell can't she get him out of her mind? There's more to her than the Louboutin wearing party-girl of previous years, however. Maybe it's time to let him in on that fact and deal with this thing between them.

LIES

By Kylie Scott
Now available.

Betty Dawsey knows that breaking things off with Thom Lange is for the best. He's nice, but boring, and their relationship has lost its spark. But steady and predictable Thom suddenly doesn't seem so steady and predictable when their condo explodes and she's kidnapped by a couple of crazies claiming that Thom isn't who he says he is.

Thom is having a hellish week. Not only is he hunting a double agent, but his fiancée dumped him, and thanks to his undercover life, she's been kidnapped.

Turns out Thom is Operative Thom and he's got more than a few secrets to share with Betty if he's going to keep her alive. With both their lives on the line, their lackluster connection is suddenly replaced by an intense one. But in his line of work, feelings aren't wanted or desired. Because feelings can be a lethal distraction.

* * * *

"You're going to break his heart."

"No, I'm not," I say. "That's sort of the whole point. If I really thought leaving him would break his heart, then I probably wouldn't be leaving him in the first place."

My best friend, Jen, does not look convinced.

Boxes fill a good half of the room. What a mess. Who knew you could accumulate so much junk in only twelve months? At least we weren't together so long that I can't remember who owns what. One year is about the sweet spot for this issue in relationships, apparently.

"The fact of the matter is, we're not in love. We have no business being engaged, let alone getting married." I sigh. "Have you seen the packing tape?"

"No. He's just such a nice guy."

"I'm not debating that." I climb to my feet, then head up the stairs to the second bedroom. Thom's unofficial workout room/home office. Not a room I normally go into. But it only takes a bit of rummaging to find what I'm looking for. Whatever else might be said about them, insurance assessors are organized. The bottom drawer of Thom's desk has a neat stash of stationery. I grab a couple rolls of thick tape.

"And leaving him this way…" Jen continues as I head back down.

"How many times have I told him we need to talk? He's always putting it off, saying it's not a good time. And now he's away again. I've been messaging him for the last week and he barely replies."

"You know he has to drop everything once a job comes up. I realize he's not the most exciting guy, Betty, but—"

"I know." I smack down a line of tape with extra zest, sealing the lid of the last box. In this Operation Abandon Ship Posthaste, I know I'm definitely slightly the bad guy. But not totally. Say sixty/forty. Or maybe seventy/thirty. It's hard to tell to what degree. "I do know all of that. But he's always busy with work or away on some business trip. What am I supposed to do?"

A sigh from Jen.

"When you realize you've made such a monumental mistake, it's hard to sit and wait to fix things. Nor is it fair on either of us to keep up the pretense."

"Guess so."

"And the fact that he's yet again made no effort to prioritize our relationship and make a little time for me in his busy schedule is just further proof that I've made the right choice in ending this now before it gets any more complicated. End of rant."

Nothing from her.

"Anyway, you're supposed to be on my side. Stop questioning me."

"You wanted to get married and have children so badly."

"Yeah." I sit back on my heels. "I blame it all on playing with Ken and Barbie's dreamhouse when I was little. But it turns out that being in a relationship with the wrong person can be even lonelier than being alone."

Jen and I have been friends since sharing a room in college. We've witnessed the bulk of each other's dating ups and downs. For some reason, I'm the type of girl who guys will go out with, but don't tend to stick with. Apparently, I'm fuckable—just not girlfriend material. Maybe it's my smart mouth. Maybe it's the whole not fitting current societal expectations of beauty i.e. I'm fat. Maybe I was born under an unlucky star. I don't know; it's their loss. Like anyone, I have my faults, but all in all, I'm awesome. And I have a lot to give. Too often in the past few months, I've had to keep reminding myself of this fact.

"There are just so many jerks out there," Jen says. "I was happy that you'd found a good one."

"I think I'd prefer a jerk who was genuinely into me than a nice guy phoning it in. Honestly, I'd rather go adopt a dozen cats and settle into old age and isolation than be with someone who treats me as if I'm an afterthought."

She looks at me for a long moment, then nods slowly. "I'm sorry it didn't work out."

"Me too."

"Time to start filling up the cars. Boy, do you owe me."

I smile. "That I do."

Jen stands and stretches before picking up one of the boxes labeled *kitchen*. "I just didn't want you to do something you'd regret, you know?"

"I know. Thank you."

Alone in the two-bedroom condo, everything is silent. My parting letter sits waiting on the coffee table with his name written on the front. A slight bulge in the envelope betrays the shape of my engagement ring. It's a sweet, simple ring. One small diamond perched on a band of yellow gold. My hand feels wrong without it. Naked. They say there are different love languages and you have to take the time to learn your partner's needs. It's like he and I never quite got there. Or maybe I'm just crappy at relationships.

The bridal magazines I'd collected are in the trash. Perhaps I should have taken them into the florist shop where I work so someone could get some use out of them. But this feels more symbolic, more definite. My family are a couple of states away, and I have only a few of what I'd classify as good friends. Being an introvert makes it hard to meet people. A boyfriend, a husband, would mean I'm no longer alone. Someone cares about me and puts me first. At least part of the time. Only Thom doesn't any of the time, so here we are.

I tighten my ponytail of long dark hair. Then, in a rare display of dexterity that my yoga instructor would be proud of, I stack three boxes in my arms and head outside into the hot afternoon sun. Jen's Honda Civic is parked at the curb, the trunk standing open as she moves things about inside. My old Subaru sits in the driveway waiting to be filled.

Birds are singing and insects chirping. It's your typical mild autumn day in California.

That's when the condo blows up behind me.

Discover 1001 Dark Nights

COLLECTION THREE
HIDDEN INK by Carrie Ann Ryan
BLOOD ON THE BAYOU by Heather Graham
SEARCHING FOR MINE by Jennifer Probst
DANCE OF DESIRE by Christopher Rice
ROUGH RHYTHM by Tessa Bailey
DEVOTED by Lexi Blake
Z by Larissa Ione
FALLING UNDER YOU by Laurelin Paige
EASY FOR KEEPS by Kristen Proby
UNCHAINED by Elisabeth Naughton
HARD TO SERVE by Laura Kaye
DRAGON FEVER by Donna Grant
KAYDEN/SIMON by Alexandra Ivy/Laura Wright
STRUNG UP by Lorelei James
MIDNIGHT UNTAMED by Lara Adrian
TRICKED by Rebecca Zanetti
DIRTY WICKED by Shayla Black
THE ONLY ONE by Lauren Blakely
SWEET SURRENDER by Liliana Hart

COLLECTION FOUR
ROCK CHICK REAWAKENING by Kristen Ashley
ADORING INK by Carrie Ann Ryan
SWEET RIVALRY by K. Bromberg
SHADE'S LADY by Joanna Wylde
RAZR by Larissa Ione
ARRANGED by Lexi Blake
TANGLED by Rebecca Zanetti
HOLD ME by J. Kenner
SOMEHOW, SOME WAY by Jennifer Probst
TOO CLOSE TO CALL by Tessa Bailey
HUNTED by Elisabeth Naughton
EYES ON YOU by Laura Kaye
BLADE by Alexandra Ivy/Laura Wright
DRAGON BURN by Donna Grant
TRIPPED OUT by Lorelei James
STUD FINDER by Lauren Blakely

On behalf of 1001 Dark Nights,

Liz Berry and M.J. Rose would like to thank ~

Steve Berry
Doug Scofield
Kim Guidroz
Jillian Stein
InkSlinger PR
Dan Slater
Asha Hossain
Chris Graham
Kasi Alexander
Fedora Chen
Jessica Johns
Dylan Stockton
Richard Blake
and Simon Lipskar

Made in the USA
Middletown, DE
25 September 2019